PAST PRAI

MW01598564

For *The Half-Life of Remorse*

"The true wizardry of *The Half-Life of Remorse* is how the random intersection of two homeless men evolves into a story of irresistible forward motion, stunning revelations, deepest human complexities and highest consequences. Underwriting this feat is Jarrett's ability to inhabit his fated characters absolutely, conjuring their voices, their minds, their wounds, their guilt, their haunted and mingled histories, with such spooky fidelity that you feel you are each one of them, and all of them, all at once. Original, gorgeous, exciting and deeply moving, *The Half-Life of Remorse* put my heart through all the paces."

—Tim Johnston, author of *New York Times* bestseller *Descent*

"Acts of searing violence transform *vulnerable lives in Grant Jarrett's* The Half-Life of Remorse. Through the anguished accounts of survivors who nearly died in that night of violence, and the delusions of one of the survivors who imagines himself capable of magic, Jarrett creates echoes of *The Tempest* and *The Winter's Tale*. This resonant novel traces the lingering effects of trauma and exposes the greatest challenge for its primary characters: self-forgiveness."

—Lee Upton, author of *The Tao of Humiliation*

"In *The Half-Life of Remorse,* Jarrett proves his mastery of narrative voice, unflinching realism, and adroit yet artful storytelling."

—Mark Wisniewski, award winning author, Best American
Short Stories and Pushcart Prize winner

For *The House That Made: Writers Reflect on the Places and People that Defined Them* (2016)

"Slim and succinct, this exquisite compilation shows how the universal nature of childhood experiences trump both cultural and geographical differences."

—*Library Journal*, Starred Review

Featured as an *Elle* magazine's "Trust Us" book, May 2016

"The essays strike a variety of tones, including curiosity, ambivalence, thoughtfulness, and earnestness. Some writers emphasize the conceit of looking at their old homes from the vantage point of a satellite. Ru Freeman and Jen Michalski, in their pieces, discuss what can be seen and what is missing in the pictures, as well as what is impossible to capture. Jeffery Renard Allen and Pamela Erens return to Chicago's North Side and South Side, respectively, to capture different aspects of the city. Other writers take readers to California, Canada, New York, and Sri Lanka. Some reexamine their families, while others consider the fragility of memory. All of the essays show, in their own ways, how homes make us and how we attempt to make homes for ourselves, at least in memory. Some readers may well be inspired to take similar journeys into the past."

—*Publishers Weekly*

"Jarrett has compiled a powerful and must-read collection of meditations on the meaning of home. Each essay in this diverse collection—with writings from rural America to war-torn Sri Lanka—transports the reader on a fresh and riveting journey into the hauntings and heartbreak of childhood. As a whole these varied voices come together in a kind of symphony, a harmonious reminder that individual stories illuminate the connection we all have to one another. Ultimately, these voices together transform this book into its own kind of shelter."

—Jennifer Percy, author of *Demon Camp*,
a *New York Times* Notable Book

For *On Ways of Leaving* (2014)

Winner of the 2014 International Book Awards in Fiction: Best New Fiction

"Ruthlessly brilliant writing brings grace to a story smoldering in pain."

—Kirkus Reviews

". . . an outstanding and devastating new novel . . ."

—Independent Publisher

THE HALF-LIFE OF REMORSE

Copyright © 2017 Grant Jarrett

Published by SparkPress, a BookSparks imprint,
A division of SparkPoint Studio, LLC
Tempe, Arizona, USA, 85281
www.gosparkpress.com

Published 2016
Printed in the United States of America
ISBN: 978-1-943006-14-4 (pbk)
ISBN: 978-1-943006-15-1 (e-bk)
Library of Congress Control Number: 2016957317

Cover design © Julie Metz, Ltd./metzdesign.com
Interior design by Tabitha Lahr

THE HALF-LIFE OF REMORSE

A NOVEL

GRANT JARRETT

SPARKPRESS

PART ONE

In the Cemetery

A HUMBLE HEADSTONE marks the grave of a man they never really knew, a man whose name they learned from the letter notifying them of his death, a letter written by a woman they've never seen, never spoken to. Now they wait there together and silently mourn his passing. She sits in her wheelchair while he stands beside her, one hand resting lightly on her shoulder. They don't speak, for what is there to say? Would he say he was a good man? Would she say that in the end he'd somehow found the strength he needed? The words would soon fade, their voices would crack and tremble, and then the tears would come. And they've both had enough of crying, enough of pain. They simply wait for this moment to run its course, for the time to be right to finally leave him behind, though in ways that cannot be expressed in words he will forever be a part of them.

Although years have passed since the last time they saw him, they will never forget the stranger who twice altered the courses of their lives. There are so many questions, but there will be no answers now. What came before his time with them will remain a mystery. There was goodness in his heart, and compassion; of this they are certain. The parasite on his conscience might have destroyed a weaker man, but he struggled, fought until it was subdued—not forgotten, but nullified, its venom purged of its potency, its thirsty roots severed. Despite the violence he was part of, his was a gentle spirit.

So they gaze down at the name on the headstone and try to understand. How had he become the man he was? And where had he found the strength, the courage to correct his life's dismal trajectory? Could they have found some way to help ease his burden? Now they will never know, but they will always wonder, until they too are dead and buried, arcane specters haunting someone else's memories.

They are weary from travel, it's getting late, and home is hours away. But still they wait. Only when the distant hills have begun to consume the ripe autumn sun do they turn to leave, their shadows stretched out before them like stick figures, gangly, skeletal, comically deformed.

And then they see her. She is limping toward them, a large woman in jeans and a plaid button-down shirt. She is holding a bouquet of flowers, lilies, snapdragons, delphinium, bells of Ireland, and daisies, as she makes her way across the cemetery lawn. Her eyes, they notice as she nears them, are slightly crossed.

"I hoped you'd come," she says.

"Yes," says the woman in the wheelchair. "Yes. Of course."

"Mary," the other woman says.

The man nods.

"You two likely have some questions. Just give me a minute to sit with him, and to put these on his grave." A sad smile illuminates her features and for a moment she is almost pretty. She kneels down and arranges the flowers on his gravestone. When they are just right, she turns to face them.

"I guess you know more than I do about what was tormenting him so. He wouldn't talk much about it, except to remind me every once in a while how much of a failure he was. Of course I knew about the two of you. I mean I sort of figured out it all had something to do with you, but that's about all I ever figured out. Maybe something he done when he was younger." This sounds more like a question than a statement.

"Can I ask *you* something, Mary?" Claire squints up at her.

"I don't see why not."

"How did he . . . you didn't say in the letter how he died. I was . . . we were just wondering—"

"Well, his heart just give out on him one morning while he was sitting at the table waiting on his fried potatoes and eggs. When I turned to set the plate in front of him, he was slouched over the table. Didn't make one single sound I could hear. For a minute I thought he'd maybe just drifted off. But then—"

Claire glances down at her legs, useless ornaments now. "How well did you know him?"

"Well enough, I guess." Mary smiles. "I married him, didn't I?"

"Oh. I didn't know . . . I wasn't aware of that."

"Course you wouldn't be. I don't imagine you heard much from him."

"No. No, nothing at all."

"Do you think you could tell me . . . what I mean is, would you be willing to explain what he did that was so awful? You would of thought he'd murdered somebody the way he sometimes got down on himself. But whenever I asked him about it, he'd just say he couldn't stand the thought of me glaring at him the way the face in the mirror sometimes did. Crude as he might of been in some of his ways, I just couldn't imagine him hurting anyone."

Claire gazes up at her father. He is old now, weary, the skin on his face slack and pleated, his eyes dull, hazy and a little distant. Someday he'll be gone and she'll be alone again with her memories. It would be comforting to have someone else to share the weight of how they were torn apart and brought back together again, someone who'd known him to carry some small part of the burden the truth has been to her, and maybe to share the joy. Even if she never saw this woman again, never spoke to her on the phone or wrote her a letter, she might not feel quite so alone. And she has asked. She wants to know, this weather-beaten woman who was married to the man whose quiet death has brought them all together. Could it be that in the end even he found love, or something like it? That would be no stranger than her own story.

"It was nothing, Mary," she finally says, and her father reaches down and squeezes her shoulder.

"I don't understand. He must of done something to make him feel like he did. He was all tore up inside." Tears glaze Mary's eyes.

"Did you . . . did he . . ." The words collide in her mouth.

"Did we love each other, two poor old rundown outcasts? Is that what you want to know?"

Claire bows her head. "I'm sorry. That wasn't very nice. And it's none of my business. I'm sorry."

"Don't be sorry." Mary chuckles. "*I'm* not. Yeah, we was in love, like a couple lazy teenagers. Even us. I wouldn't of married him if we hadn't been."

Claire draws a deep breath and looks into the other woman's eyes. "I'm glad," she says and smiles. "He didn't do anything, Mary. He just did his best. He did the best he could."

PART TWO

Seven years earlier

CHAPTER 1

Chick

NO QUESTION ABOUT IT, the old son of a bitch is nuts. Course, I ain't sure how much difference that makes out here where nothing makes much sense, and I guess I ain't about to be hired as poster child for perfect mental health neither, but he's in a whole different class from me. Course then I guess there's worse things than being loopy. Funny thing is, I mostly tend to trust him. He's got more than a couple screws rattling around in that scraggly head of his, but so far as I can tell, he's never tried to swindle me out of nothing. Not that I ever had much anybody'd want. Still in all, I've met some guys would pry out your molars for the soggy bread wads they could scoop out of them, but then I just don't figure him for that kind of behavior. Plus which, the son of a bitch has somehow weaseled hisself a real fine spot in this shit-hole of a town, and that ain't nothing to scoff at, specially with the weather so damn changeable these days.

First time I run into him we was both waiting on the traffic signal over Sixth and Main. I'm just standing there minding my own business and balling up the lint in my overcoat's one good pocket when he all of a sudden clears his throat and growls, "Turn green or a pestilence on your goats," or some high-toned gobbledygook such as that. Course the light *does* finally change, but then it's got to change sometime or other if it ain't froze up. But he looks over at me, all proud with his chest pushed out, and announces in that raspy buzz saw voice of his, "I guess *that* got his goat." Well I got no answer to that one, so I just scurry on my way, not looking back but hoping he ain't following behind.

About a week or two after that I got a good half a cigarette hanging out my mouth. The thing's pretty near dry, but I can't for the life of me find nothing to light it up with. I'm about ready to pitch a nic fit when he strides on over from behind a bush or under a hedge or whatever and flicks open this old chrome Zippo and lights me up. I say thanks, and I *do* appreciate it, but I just can't take my peepers off that lighter. Had me one just like it when I was fourteen, maybe fifteen, way back around 1960 or so. Hung on to it for a couple of years too, as best I can recall, but somewhere along the line the thing just up and vanished on me. So anyways, I guess he sees me gawking, cause he looks at me with them eyebrows dropping down like a pair of storm clouds over them beady eyes and says, all spooky and low, "I can see the hunger in your visage." Now, while he stares at me like a scientist inspecting some new germ he's trying to figure out a use for, I ponder on what the hell that's supposed to mean. I mean, is he referring to the Zippo or my empty stomach or something else entirely? Finally I says to him, "I'll just take your word on that one, Farley," or something like it. He just snaps the lighter shut and slips it back into his own grimy pant pocket.

Well, for a good minute or so the two of us stands there eyeing one the other, me puffing on my piece of cigarette and him just deliberating I suppose. But he's got a kind of gleamy look on his face, and I figure maybe he wants a toke. We're all in pretty much the same boat out here and we find comfort where and when we can, so I hand him what's left of my butt and he takes the longest, profusest draw on that thing I seen in my life. That wrinkly paper draws back over a big old glowing ash and before I know it he's down to the goddamn filter and the ash jumps ship and there ain't no more smoke nor fire to be seen.

"Shit," I say, more than a little frustrated cause I ain't hardly got a chance to smoke it myself and I only meant for him to have one regular-type drag rather than suck the entire future out of it. What's he do? He reaches a hand on into his other pocket and pulls out half a cold hamburger what looks like it spent a week or two soaking up weather and abuse on some major highway and aims the ratty thing right at me.

Truth is, if I never see another cold hamburger it'll be pretty soon, but I imagine it's mostly the gesture what counts, so I take the floppy, squished-up thing and kind of pick at the bun until he ain't paying attention and then slip it into my own pocket, the one with the hole so big a basketball'd slip through it without scraping the sides. We stand there for a while longer, not saying much, ducking behind the bushes whenever the patrol car comes scooting by, and before you know it the rain's pouring down like a tall cow pissing on a flat rock. That's when he locks them eyes on me and says, "Have you a secure and tranquil place to rest your head?" or such high-caliber terminology as that. That's just the way he talks. My first thinking on the topic is, this here geezer's some thief or maybe even a sex pervert out to try and make me do things I wouldn't even care to think about or see pictures of. You have enough direct dealings with human beings and you can't help but think that way after a while. But then I think, yeah, maybe so, but maybe *not* so, which means maybe I'd do well to survey the situation and see what I might make of it. I guess I ain't near as fit as I used to of been, and I was never much of a fighter, but by the look of him he's some years older and kind of stringy and stooped over to boot, so I figure I can get the best of him in mortal combat if the occasion was to arise, though I'm generally inclined to go some distance to avoid that sort of thing. And anyways, I ain't going to nod out in his vicinity till I know right from up and down from left.

Well, the final conclusion is the old guy's found hisself a handy little space under the raised staircase out back of the church up there on Decker. Says nobody else knows of it, and I figure he's right about that. Anyways, that's the long and short of how it is me and Sam come to be roommates.

CHAPTER 2

Sam

THERE WOULD BE LITTLE point and no pleasure in attempting to delineate the series of misfortunes that led to my downfall. Even if I felt compelled to do so, it would most likely prove impossible. My memories have grown increasingly fluid and my perspective may be skewed. For now, let's just say that when my potency began to diminish, as, in retrospect, I suppose was inevitable, I was not emotionally equipped to accept it. It is no easy feat to adjust to earthly limitations after spending a dozen lifetimes virtually unconstrained. Perhaps it's akin to what any man feels when, after years of good health and vigor, he is finally confronted with illness, incapacitation, and the prospect of an end he's spent a lifetime tacitly disregarding. The thought of facing life on its own terms, and death, was very nearly too much for me to endure. Consequently, instead of preparing to wind down and pass my remaining years in relative comfort among the mortals, I sought to stave off my descent, or simply ignore it. And yet with the passage of time and the daily disappointments, I ultimately had no choice but to surrender to the physical manifestations of senescence. When it was probably already too late, I made a couple unenthusiastic and ultimately futile attempts to recover my balance in hopes of finding a tranquil setting in which to come to terms with my quotidian destiny. To that end I labored in the stockroom of a shoe store for a few weeks, in a reeking tavern for a month or so, on the assembly line in a plumbing fittings factory for what seemed an eternity. And there were other enterprises too, many difficult and disagreeable, but of course it was all for naught.

Some three hundred or three thousand years ago, just before in a sudden blinding seizure my dissolution began, I might have snapped my fingers and conjured a cushy milieu in which to while away my waning years. I might have invoked a mansion in the mountains, a castle overlooking some sun-blanched Spanish beach. Instead, I continued to behave as though I were immortal, as though I had a boundless future in which to frolic from one corner of the universe to another. Yes, before the cataclysm, I flitted about this canted globe and far beyond. Afterward I was virtually immobilized, rendered impotent by some amorphous burden, or perhaps simply by the knowledge of my demotion to what I could only view as *mere* humanity.

What I failed to realize then, and still have difficulty fully accepting, is that perhaps this is what life, *any life,* is, a struggle we endure simply to prolong the struggle, and that it is within this context alone that we must attempt to find our purpose, our cause, our joy or passion, whatever it is that helps us sustain the belief, fallacious or not—a distinction of diminishing relevance—that somehow we matter. It may be that this need, to feel valuable, is what drives most sentient beings, what enables them to go on when going on seems impossible.

And so it wasn't long before I began to mute my anguish with cigarettes and alcohol, and I gradually grew lax in my personal hygiene. I would go for weeks without sleep and then lie comatose for days on end. The truth is I've even spent some time in confinement, dank, gloomy cells where the bedclothes contained more nutritional value, and were more appetizing, than the meals, and where the nocturnal vermin were treated with more humanity and respect than the invited residents. I don't doubt there are more than a few years that I cannot recollect. I suppose even a faded wizard is subject to the indignities of senility. And yet, although it makes no sense to me, I've had a vague feeling these last few months that there is something I must do if I am to pass from this whirling orb in peace. My fear is that this is just a desperate concoction of my subconscious, an illusion I've contrived to delude myself into believing there is some reason to go on. Either way, I am prepared to embrace it.

And perhaps that very need for a sense of purpose was at least a part of my motivation for taking in this peculiar orphan who calls himself Chick.

CHAPTER 3

Chick

MIND YOU, I DIDN'T sleep so sound that first night with that furry old loon twitching and snoring about a creepy arm's length away. But since then you might say me and Sam's become fast friends, least as much as you can be friends with a nutcase who thinks he's some kind of magician or wizard. I figure if he can dig up a private room under some rickety old steps and drum up half a bottle of stale rotgut now and again or a greasy chicken wing, and he don't do me no bodily harm I can attest to, well then, I could do a good bit worse for company. And I figure everybody on this Earth needs some kind of company, like it or not.

Now, do I sometimes still worry maybe he's going to all of a sudden blow a brain gasket and hack my head off with a cleaver or rip out my innards with some rusty old scissors while I'm sleeping off a drunk? I'll admit I've thought on it once or twice, but I imagine if he was going to do something like that he would of did the dirty deed and hightailed it out of Muncie by now, that is if anybody took notice. For better or worse, my noggin's still right about where it's always been, so I figure he ain't planning do me no hurt. Fact is I got a feeling he's as partial to me as you can be to anybody when you're convinced you're Houdini or Cognac the Magnificent.

On another topic altogether, I just now noticed I'm in drastic need of a bath. When you can't stand the smell of your own self, you can pretty well bet there's others out there who's noticed it with something less than admiration. Course I'm used to folks heading on over to the other side of the street when they see me loitering in their path, though with them little screens they're all the time staring at they don't see much of nothing these days, but I hate like hell to have some innocent soul get a whiff of me a block and a half away and turn around and have to find another way wherever they're going or just give it up and head back home where it's safe till the danger's passed. Still in all, it's tougher than you might think trying to get a good cleanup when you're living like this. It's almost like people want to be able to pick you out easy so there ain't no question just who to look down on.

CHAPTER 4

Claire

EVERY TIME I THINK I've finally given up, I glimpse someone who bears a vague resemblance to him, or to what I can recall of him. Sometimes it's the thick head of hair—hair that was always a little unruly—at other times it might be his self-assured walk, head held up, chest and chin thrust proudly forward. Of course it's never him. And the truth is that those anonymous men who for a hopeful moment capture the tattered periphery of my imagination are always much younger than he would be. In spite of all the time that's passed, I can only envisage the man I knew, though his image seems to erode a little more every day in spite of the precious photographs that remain. I guess somewhere deep inside I know I'll never see my father again, but knowing it won't happen and abandoning the dream are not quite the same thing, are they?

CHAPTER 5

Sam

BASED UPON HIS SHABBY appearance and the incongruous diversity in the patchwork of his discourse, I'd say that Chick is a seasoned derelict, though at times it seems he's not as conversant in the vicissitudes of street life as one might expect of someone with his years in its thrall. Perhaps he's not terribly bright, though human intelligence can take different forms and lie in unexpected places. Still, in spite of his peculiarities, I find him an entertaining, sometimes even a comforting companion. And who am I to judge this ragged stranger? Like myself, he must have his own tale to tell. And though I don't yet fully trust him, I have a sense that he is at heart a decent man. Indeed, there is the feeling, or at least the illusion of security, even kinship in our unlikely alliance.

And yet it's evident he questions my veracity. But why shouldn't he? After all, he's only mortal. Of course he hasn't seen what I'm capable of—well, what I *was* capable of only a couple dozen years ago. Has it been that long? Longer? It's all begun to run together like sludge in the city gutters.

I suppose I might work some minor incantation in order to prove myself to him, to all of them, but that would be beneath me—a tacit acknowledgement that after hundreds of years, or however long I've been alive now, it's all over but the final fizz, and frankly I have no wish to squander what little strength I might still possess merely to satisfy these unimaginative skeptics. As unlikely as it now seems, I might yet be called upon to employ my remaining powers for something more crucial than a public confirmation of that which I already know to be true. I can only hope that if such a thing arises I am up to the task. Until then, let them think what they will. Their skepticism cannot alter who and what I am, or what I was. And I was something.

Some of my fondest recollections, hazy though they are, are those of my flashier, more flamboyant feats, the ones designed simply to extract gasps of joy from the gaggle of wide-eyed children in whose presence I performed them. I don't doubt that there are those among my thaumaturgical brethren who take the greatest pride in those feats that have altered the earthen landscape or diverted the course of events, and while I can understand that, what has remained with me after all this time are the expressions of incredulity and delight on those cherubic faces as they gazed upon some miracle I'd set into action, bending and twisting the very laws of nature with a mere gesture. Those clear eyes, open wide, reflecting fireworks I'd ignited for their eager eyes alone, have continued to sustain me in these destitute declining years, in the dark, cold nights under rattling bridges or in misty cornfields, surrounded by a mystifying mingling of nocturnal hums, howls, rustles, murmurs, chirps, and clicks—sounds whose provenance a timid man, or a wise one, would be hesitant to investigate. And I am eternally grateful for that.

CHAPTER 6

Chick

CHICK AIN'T MY REAL name, of course. Given name's Barry, Barry Munson. Took a lot of ribbing as a kid about my initials being B.M., but somewhere along the line somebody or other was thoughtful enough to hang that moniker on me and it just sort of stuck. Now Chick's pretty much the only name anybody calls me, not to say too many folks bother to call me anything at all, at least nothing I'd want to repeat.

Now, I got a pretty good idea what I must look like to your more upstanding folks, what they most likely think when I come hobbling down the sidewalk in my trussed-up shoes and baggy old trousers hanging on by nothing more than a pretzeled paper clip and a sizable helping of distress. I suppose I'd think pretty much the same thing if I was in their shiny new floor-shines. And I ain't blaming nobody else for where I ended up neither. Truth is I never been much to speak of, not from day one. Hell, even my own mom and dad could see that. Reminded me of it pretty regular too, just in case it'd slipped my mind.

Not like old Sam. Now there's a guy's been something, though if you know what that something is, you're one or two up on me—and him too I'd wager. But you can plainly see, what with his speech and manner, the old trash sifter's got education and worldly

28

wisdom to boot. Maybe he was some kind of judge, or maybe a doctor or a scientist or lawyer or something of the like. He ain't no magical wizard, but I will say he's smart as a whip. You can tell it by listening to him talk. That is when he ain't jawing about this or that whammy or some other cockeyed fairy tale.

As for me, long as I can recollect I've always kind of went my own way, maybe not so much by choice as what you might call happenstance. Hated school for the most part, or maybe it was more like *it* hated *me*, at least the teachers and most of the other kids did. And I wasn't much interested in any work I ever put my hands to, though I tried most any manual labor you could name least once or twice, from house painting and your basic carpenter work to farming to factory work to truck driving, ditch digging, and road construction. Guess I do have a knack for fixing mechanical things when someone gives me a chance, which they usually don't, so it ain't been much use to me nor anyone else. Parents wasn't too bad when they was sober or not hungover, but when that might of been I'm hard-pressed just now to recall. Anyways, I took what work I could get and kept moving for most of my years. Guess there ain't nothing else I know. Truth is, but for the cold and the hunger, it ain't so bad as what you might expect. Well, that and the lonesomeness, which is sort of like a hunger a nice hot homemade meal won't lay a glove on.

Now, do I ever wonder what I might of been if circumstance otherwise allowed? Well, Mister, I will not deny it. There's a whole slew of things I never got a chance to take a crack at. But what's the use of might-of-beens and incriminations? Old Sam says, "A man's as noble as his finest instincts and as wicked as his worse infraction." He says we're all everything all balled up, some tighter than others. I ain't entirely sure I fully understand what he's aiming at, but it has a fine enough sound to satisfy my needs, so I figured to latch onto it for the occasional usage. I don't guess he'd much mind. I ain't so sure he'd know where he heard it before.

True fact is, every once in a while for just a minute or two I get the feeling maybe some little part of him ain't quite so loco as he most generally appears. Course then a half a minute later he's yapping about filling the sky with flying stars and breathing fire and making volcanoes and powering a city with a piece of goddamn citrus fruit or some crazy-ass shit. It's just about that time that I goes to myself—cause what's the point of saying it aloud and getting him all flustrated—I goes, "Sure as shit stinks the worst when it's fresh and steamy, the old coot's as batty as a goddamn chicken with its head blazing and a firecracker jammed up its fine-feathered butt."

CHAPTER 7

Sam

ALTHOUGH I WAS UNAWARE of it, I had forgotten how to laugh. Perhaps it wasn't the capacity for joy that perished, but the will to experience it. And look who has assisted in its recovery: an inveterate vagrant, a mendicant who for all I know would fleece his own forgotten mother for a mouthful of bourbon and half a cigarette. I, who skipped and danced among the moons of Jupiter; I, who skated around the icy rings of Saturn; I, who drew life from the merciless grip of death, have come to this. Pish! Life was far simpler, and far less anguished, when I wasn't so damned lucid. But here I am, clear as the Mercury sky in summer. Enough!

Yesterday, after a week or more of idle threats, the sky let loose with a deafening vengeance, and when the parturient clouds finally cracked open they gave birth to a drenching that raged from early morning through the afternoon and continued well into the evening hours. It was cold and damp under these church steps, and we had nothing but a bag of stale hamburger buns to eat and the water that dripped through the rotting boards above us, collected in a colorful collection of old whiskey bottles and soda cans, to slake our reluctant thirst. Although we passed the majority of the stormy day in silence, playing cards with a partial deck, I believe I learned a little more about my new compatriot.

31

It seems that, in spite of his appearance and his apparent familiarity with the meager trappings of this life, and despite a long and undoubtedly colorful history of criminality and vice, he possesses his own set of standards, however abstruse. Perhaps I wouldn't trust him with my billfold, if I owned one, but I don't divine in him the intrinsic malevolence I've found in many of the more fortunate and better educated souls I've encountered. I only hope I have not misjudged him, but even if I have, he, like me, is one of the lost and forgotten, and who else is willing to look us in the eye and listen to what we have to say, to reach out a hand and help us up when we've fallen, to try to understand? Who among the more fortunate is willing to even risk coming that close?

Addiction, inherited poverty, mental illness, stupidity, poor education, or none at all, minor misfortune or grand catastrophe, ignorance, laziness, and poor training: these are just a few of the numerous routes to life on the street. And the rules we live by, most of which are subject to adjustment whenever self-preservation, or even convenience, requires it, are as varied as our paths. The crippled and ill are everywhere you look, and you cannot help but feel for them, and then, when the realization finally crystallizes that those poor souls may reflect your own bleak future, for yourself. Some are crippled inside, where it isn't always immediately apparent, though if you allow yourself to, and if they let you come near enough, you can often sense it. And then there are those who wear the mark of death, whose bodies have risen up against them, assaulted from within or without. The aspect of death washes over their once smooth and even features, seeming to ravage them before your eyes, dragging them toward their dark, lonely graves. Many, I suspect, are gripped by drug addiction or by that wretched virus that seemed to sprout up from nowhere, the very life siphoned out of them, their once strong bodies looted by the relentless assault of ravenous bacteria, suicidal invaders who colonize and then annihilate their plunder. Do they, the bacteria, then die? I can only hope they do, and that it is, for them, an agonizing end. Of course that wouldn't alter a thing. But how do these doomed and deadly children find their way to this grim penultimate chapter? Could it be that they too are fallen wizards? It seems unlikely, but then the longer I live the less logic and sense I seem to find in the world around me. Or maybe I can no longer discern the difference between logic and random, mindless chaos.

And yet, to me the most terrifying of all are the cold-eyed, willfully savage inhabitants of this dismal existence, those who seem somehow to have been born into malevolence, those who take pleasure in causing pain. And it isn't fear for my own well-being that terrifies me so much as the knowledge that humans such as these can exist, empathy and innocence apparently omitted at their very conception, or ripped from them at an age when they were still tender enough to feel and malleable enough to mold. Of course we are all selfish at the core. We need to be, though there is a kind of selfishness that serves the individual without destroying the society within which he exists. But to these people nothing has value but what they want at a given moment, not even their own lives. And when you have nothing to lose, you have immense power over those who do value life. When you add physical strength or ingenuity, a touch of malice or sadism, you've got something deadly and malign. And this I simply cannot comprehend. And it chills my blood and tears at the ragged strands of my remaining hope.

CHAPTER 8

Chick

Truth is I've lied and I've cheated and I've stole and I've done far worse than that too. The worst of the damage I done's a frittered lifetime behind me now, but it's never so far from my mind I can't get froze up all over again just thinking back on it, and that kind of cold you can't smoke out with a hundred garbage can fires and a tanker truck full of cheap bourbon, though I sure as shit have tried. And I suppose I'll keep trying long as I'm hanging on. Sure, I was young and scared and maybe I wasn't never taught no better, but that don't alter the facts one bit. Once something's done it can't be undone. Man can't change what he's done, or what he is for all that. I got no delusions about the harm I caused.

At the same time I don't guess I feel too terrible for any number of minor activities another fella mightn't readily admit to in polite company. I can't say as I feel too choked up about lifting an occasional can of chicken soup or chocolate bar or bottle of Jack, and though I'll admit it took some getting used to, I don't lose too much sleep on account of the times some more upright citizen's left something valuable right out where I was forced into a moral dilemma that's a touch too sticky for the likes of me. That's like slapping a bloody old beefsteak in front of some starving hound dog and expecting him to sit all calm and composed, whistling and filing his nails. I'll be damned if he don't chomp on to that wad of meat and make quick work of it too. He's only human, and to my way of thinking that ain't no compliment.

What frightens me now is that I'm starting to feel right at home with old Sam. I'm not saying I begun to buy into that happy horseshit about spells and all, but I say there's more to him than bone, gristle, and some of the nastiest-smelling breath you'll find on a two-legged beast what ain't dying or dead already, in which case why the hell is it breathing?

Now on that particular score, I figure something wicked must of got all tangled up in his gullet a couple-few years back and it's been rotting and decaying right there where it set up shop ever since, delivering free of charge the most deadliest fumes a man's ever breathed in and lived to tell the tale. And the truth is, old Sam strikes me to be the kind of fella where if he knew how terrible he was polluting the neighborhood he'd be all embarrassed and upset and want to rectify it too.

Maybe for other folks the sense of smell serves some sort of useful purpose—though what that might be I'm hard-pressed to say—but after years of poking through garbage dumpsters, wearing the same third- and fourth-hand clothes for months at a time, crouching in parking lots to take a dump, and living around other folks what got no soap or deodorant, it'd be the first I'd give up and no two ways about it. And do it with a wink and a grin.

Why, to my mind folks smelling bad may be the most convincing argument against the idea of a God anyone ever come up with. I mean what kind of almighty what's-it would go creating humans and then think to himself, "Hey, I know, I'll make them smell something awful when they ain't washed for a week or so. Won't that be a pleasant convenience?" Fact is it's easier to explain why a God might make death and pain and suffering than them awful bodily odors. At least death and pain could maybe teach a person something and make them think about how others might feel and to be careful and so forth. Making folks stink just seems like some kind of nasty joke nobody laughs at cause when you laugh you got no choice but to breathe in. What kind of God would come up with that?

But then if there ain't a God and that revolutionary stuff with the monkeys and whatnot is where we come from, there'd still have to be some reason for it, at least the way I heard it explained. Now you might say a bad smell is a sort of signal so you know you're dirty and need some cleaning up, but that don't wash cause the main reason you need to get clean is so you don't *stink* no more, which you wouldn't *need* to if you wasn't made to stink in the first place. I mean, far as I can tell the bad smell is the worst part of being dirty, well that and the itching and chafing, so if it was made to let you know you was dirty, that was some backward-ass planning, making up a problem for no reason but so you could know you have the problem and then solve it and be back to square one until a day or a week later. The damned thing wouldn't of even been a problem in the first place if you didn't have to know about it.

Now, I imagine some folks would say your sense of smell helps you figure out what's safe to eat and what's not, but that idea goes to hell in a handcart as soon as you get within a couple hundred feet of a pot of boiling brussels sprouts, which people swears is good for you but which makes me feel like I'm about to puke up my whole insides and all their various attachments too. My mom cooked them up once to punish me I think, but I run out of the house holding my breath and didn't go back for a couple days for fear the leftovers would do me in. She only did it that one time cause my father said they give him a bad headache and the dry heaves too. Said he thought she was boiling a sickly rat but I figured that'd smell a touch better than them sprout things and probably be more appetizing too.

CHAPTER 9

Sam

I'VE HAD MY SHARE OF disquieting dreams, dreams that felt particularly potent or real, dreams whose connection to me was either obscure or nonexistent. But the images that have flashed across my consciousness as I've begun to drift off in recent days seem borrowed from some stranger's life. They aren't dreams exactly, but shadowy shreds of what appears to be a single night in his life. They lack the crystal clarity of my waking ruminations, the almost palpable quality of my more honestly acquired recollections of magnificent feats facilely performed and bloody battles halted with the wave of a hand or the wink of an eye. But they possess a more pungent flavor, a more enduring aftertaste.

When first they manifested themselves, I dismissed these visions as mere cerebral poltergeists tormenting my subconscious, perhaps provoked by a less than ideal diet, or possibly a response to living in such close proximity to a relative stranger—a most peculiar phrase. When they continued and I gradually became aware of a certain homogeneity, my curiosity was enkindled. Increasingly, and a little disturbingly, I've developed a distant feeling for the faceless apparition whose memories I suspect I've unwittingly purloined, a growing fascination with these foreboding moments rent from his thoughts. Though I sense he is a younger man, I really know nothing about him, and yet he seems so real that I've come to care for him. Does he now remember missing moments from *my* past or is this all just the whimsy of a mischievous and increasingly senile mind?

But what if it is not the stranger's past, but a hint of his future to which I bear witness? What if this muddle of images is a portent and I am being summoned to rescue him from some impending peril, my final act of wizardry before the endless darkness envelops me and my brittle bones are finally laid to rest. How can I know? Pish! This impotency is agonizing, this desperate need for a sense of purpose an illusionist nonpareil.

CHAPTER 10

Claire

ASIDE FROM THE MEMORIES of the family that was stolen from me, my students are just about all I have now. And in their way, even *they* represent a kind of connection to the distant past. My father loved his work as a grade school principal almost as much as he loved time with his family, and, with one or two notable exceptions, he loved the children at his school almost as much as he loved his own. There's no doubt that my face is my mother's—anyone who knew her can see that—but when I gaze up at a cloudless night sky and see the stars twinkling I can still see the sparkle in my father's eyes, the look of wonder he always wore when educating us about the stars and planets, about the universe, about anything. Sometimes, when he spoke to us afterward about what we'd seen, Timmy and I would hold hands and close our eyes, and for a few minutes it was almost as though we were actually visiting those distant worlds.

Timmy and I. Another phrase that's lost its meaning, a barbed vestige of my former life, an endless, stabbing reminder of all that was lost, not just to me, but to all of us. I am little more than the scar that remains.

CHAPTER 11

Chick

I NEVER WOULD OF THOUGHT when I was a kid I'd be all but begging for a place to wash up in, or dipping some frizzy-headed toothbrush I snatched a couple months ago from Mr. Rexall in a three-dollar fifth of whiskey and going at what's left of my pearly grays like a pup scratching at a squadron of fleas. Seems to me a man will get used to near anything, and I'm no exception, but he'll also hang on to a scrap of whatever it is he figures makes him a man till he's sucking in his last breath.

Last night the two of us was lying back in the candlelight, jawing about nothing and finishing the backwash in a can of Pabst I come across in my evening travels. Well, after we ain't said nothing for a long stretch of time, I glanced on over at old Sam. His eyes was shut, as far as I could tell, but his lips was flapping under that furry beard of his like a couple of bait worms on a dusty riverbank. I don't know if he's dreaming or trying to notify me of something, so I go, "If you're blathering in my direction, Farley, I'm afraid I ain't getting your message." All of a sudden, his shoulders rattle and his eyes flash wide open and he turns that gleamy gaze of his on me and says, "I've been witnessing a scene from another person's life," or some such perfumed horseshit as that. Course I got no answer to that one, never having heard its like before, so I just stare back at him for a time, I guess hoping he'll offer some explanation or just nod off and be quiet. But then I think, it can't do me no harm to listen to the old fuzz-bucket, plus which he can be kind of entertaining when he gets on one of his wizardly rants, long as you don't start taking him serious. So I slap on my thoughtful face and pinch at my chin for a second and say, all curious-like, "Hmm. That so?"

What I come to find is he's all in a state cause of some person whose head he thinks he's somehow weaseled his way inside of. Now this don't seem quite like his normal wizard blusteration to me, and I can see by looking at him he's shook up pretty good, but I don't know should I sit back and listen till he gets the disillusions out of his system, or hightail it out of there before his scraggly old head pops open and the regiment of hungry hamsters what's been gnawing away at his brain comes scurrying out in search of another light snack. Long and short of it is he's convinced he's been peering right inside this other fella's life, though I'm wondering whether he mightn't be better off trying to untangle his *own* rusty internal workings before he goes worrying about some imaginary lunatic.

So while I'm still trying to absorb the sum and substance of his ramblings, he tells me how there must be some kind of important reason why he's visioning this guy. It's all just bits and pieces of stuff and it's kind of blurry, he tells me, but it's coming clearer every day, which to my mind can't be classified what you want to rush out and call great news.

Now to be honest, all I can rightly think—to myself of course, cause I don't see no reason to tell the old gasbag he's beginning to drift some—all I can think is, he might of finally found hisself a ticket to the local loony bin. Course that's when I realize that'd most probably be a return ticket, and well overdue at that.

I won't say I didn't sleep none, cause that'd be a lie, but I will confess I waited till he sawed a couple cords of firewood before I finally begun to relax enough to shut both of my own eyes all at once.

CHAPTER 12

Sam

WHEN I AWOKE THIS morning, I heard sniffles and staggered inhalations, alien sounds issuing from where my new companion was sprawled out on his crinkled cradle of last week's headlines, advertisements, opinions, and obituaries. Chick was lying on his side with his back turned toward me, and I could swear the man was sobbing.

My impulse was to reach out to him, of course, to offer him succor, but I fear it has been too long for both of us since last we were glanced by any expression of tenderness, affection, or even genuine concern. So in spite of my increasing fondness for the poor, lost lad, I simply could not bring myself to console him. Did I lose more than my magic those endless years ago? Did I also lose the greater part of my soul, or is it just timid and a tad sluggish from so long a dormancy? One can only hope that the capacity to comfort those in need is not the sort of attribute that can be permanently excised from a man's soul. Or a wizard's.

It's easy to forget when encountering our fellow travelers that there is much more to them than their surfaces might reveal. The fact is that a human being is far and away the most complex, the most mysterious entity in this boundless universe. I suppose all men have histories of loss and disappointment; all men have

42

known moments of joy and jubilation. And yet no matter how great our powers of perception, we can never perceive the full depth of another man's character, the magnitude of his joy, the acuteness of his pain or his fear. We can stand at a comfortable distance and make our pronouncements and judgments based on the little we see, which only narrows our view and blurs our vision, but we can never truly know.

A wizard's life is not perfect, but I suppose it is close enough. Nevertheless, even I am not wholly immune, particularly in these final years, to human frailties, to fear and sadness and physical pain, and to a distant melancholy that seems to creep nearer with each new day. I, too, know something of the darkness that can lurk within a human heart, if not its provenance.

It just seems such a bitter irony to have once been capable of so much and now to be impotent to soothe a needy comrade. I am mocked by age, scorned by weakness, and degraded by fear. I was once as a god, but now I am barely a man. And Chick is not the only one who stands to suffer for my weakness, my impotence. There is someone else calling out to me, a little louder every day, the man whose life has somehow intersected mine, a man in turmoil, I fear, invoking a pale wizard who cannot even bring himself to grip the trembling shoulder of a troubled companion.

The bitter truth is that the planets are gradually fading, the fiery battles running together in the fluid shadows of my memory. My magnificent past is becoming little more than a murky dream inhabited by blurry specters that dwindle a little more each day. And without the sorcery, without the resplendent displays, the thunder and the raging storms I manifested, without the glory I possessed, what would I be? But it's really too late for that question, isn't it? There are other, more pertinent questions to ask now. What is it that I have become? And what, if anything, could possibly lie ahead for one such as me? I suppose I'm merely waiting for my body and mind to accept what my heart already knows.

CHAPTER 13

Claire

IF ONLY I COULD LET IT GO. Then maybe I could claim whatever remains of my life. Surely I deserve that. That can't be too much to ask, can it, to be complete, of some value to the world? Perhaps just too much to expect.

On the other hand, it might be that letting the past go would be more painful than continuing to hold on to it. Maybe I'm clinging to the pain, holding on for dear life. As if I even had a choice.

CHAPTER 14

Chick

NOT THAT IT EXCUSES nothing, but I was just a teenager when it all went to shit. I was hanging around with Lenny and Phil, a couple older guys who occasionally bought me and a couple of other lowlife kids beer and whiskey at a sizeable profit, cause we was too young and too cowardly to traipse into a bar or a liquor store and try to buy our own. These two guys for some reason or another took a liking to me, and pretty soon the three of us started hanging out maybe once or twice a week. Usually, we'd down a few beers at Lenny's first, cause he had his own place, and then we'd go strolling into this or that store and spread out like we was doing some serious shopping. Then, while two of us kept them busy with all manner of questions and the like, the other one's stuffing his baggy old overcoat with whatever he could lay his paws onto. Other times, we'd liberate batteries or hubcaps or now and again even wheels and tires from some car we happen to come across in our late night travels. There was this one guy over in Wilkes-Barre who'd buy a good amount of the car stuff from us and then sell it out of his Esso gas station.

We done other stuff we shouldn't of too. When we was drinking or when I was drinking and they was drinking plus getting high on pot or diet pills or the like, Len and Phil'd act a little crazy, and sometimes I'd get kind of scared, though I don't figure I ever let on—least I tried like hell not to. I knew clear enough what we was doing wasn't right or legal neither, and I didn't feel no sense of pride about that, but I was making what you'd call pocket money and I was acting tough, like I figured a man was supposed to act if he wanted to get anywhere in life. And plus, most kids— kids who would of razzed me before cause of my ratty, second- hand clothes or my homemade haircut—they wouldn't say "boo" to me now cause they figured I was some kind of hoodlum, and I guess I didn't mind that all too much neither.

I had a pretty clear idea these two guys wasn't the best com- pany I could of chose, but they was friendly enough to me for the most part when others wasn't and they sort of took me in when most guys their age wouldn't of pissed on my head if my ears was shooting bright blue flames and I was screaming out for help. And they brung some drama and excitement into my dull world. Still in all, with what we done, we never once got caught, and when we got into scuffles nobody got more than a bloody nose or a little cut of the blade. Leastwise not till that one horrible night.

It was already late and we was drinking pretty heavy, plus which Lenny and Phil was likely doing a shitload more than that, cause they was starting to get about as crazy-eyed and wild as I ever seen them, either one. It was Phil who started talking about finally getting out of the small-time, as he was fond of calling it. He said we wasn't nothing more than penny-ante hoodlums and we ought to make our mark and make some real money all at once. I was never much asked for my personal opinion, so I just set there and listened, but truth is, I was getting a little wound up myself, seeing myself like some television bad guy, with the shiny dark hair and the mustache and fancy clothes and maybe a long, sleek convertible with some long, sleek lady to go with it. Anyways, Len says how he don't fully disagree with what Phil was getting at, but the question was, what did he have in mind? Not much more than a minute later, Phil jumps up and lets out a hoot and a holler and he announces, "We're going to make us a mark, boys." Turns out he's ready to head out right then and there and break into some houses where folks is sleeping or away on vacation. Just go to some quiet neighborhood where nothing ever goes on, he says, and creep on in to some dark house and grab all we can lay our paws to. He figures we can park his creaky old Dodge wagon in a alley somewhere nearby and stock her up with cash and cameras and silver and who knows what and still get out of there before anybody knows what's what.

Like I already said, I was getting all caught up in the mood, but still in all, I was mostly figuring it wasn't going to come to nothing more than a little chin music in the end, and frankly I was glad *of* it.

Course then, I was wrong. I was about as wrong as a person can be.

CHAPTER 15

Claire

CONSIDERING ALL THAT happened when I was a child, I suppose my life is reasonably good. I have a regular job—a job that on most days I truly cherish—I'm physically comfortable in spite of my handicap, I'm no longer haunted by nightmares, and though I still entertain occasional thoughts of suicide, I seem finally to have gotten through the worst of my once debilitating depression. I don't generally socialize unless I feel I must, but I'm blessed with a small circle of close friends—as close as I'll allow, that is—and most of my colleagues respect me, or seem to, which is good enough for me. There has been no real romance for me, but from what I've seen in my adult life, romance is a dubious commodity, and seldom to be relied upon in the long term. That I don't, and won't have a child, is by far my greatest disappointment, outside of my early losses. But that too, I have come to begrudgingly accept. Or at least I believe I have.

Certainly I haven't forgotten how I got here, but somehow I have endured. And yet I can't deny that the life I've made for myself is less than complete. It's as though there is this hollow space inside me, hollow but bitterly cold with echoes of some happier time bouncing endlessly, mockingly off the icy walls.

CHAPTER 16

Sam

WHEN I AWOKE LATE THIS morning, my new roommate was already out gallivanting about, so I took advantage of the opportunity and made an effort to tidy up our little hovel under the church steps. It's really quite cramped in here, even for one grown man, and always either dusty or damp. And of course there's no heat or air conditioning, no plumbing or electricity, but it is as private, indeed as welcoming, as any place I've laid my head in a decade or more. I suppose, now that I've elected to share it, that the likelihood of discovery, followed by a swift, embarrassing, and possibly violent eviction, has increased. Still, I cannot now imagine casting him out, and I know well enough that, although it was I who unearthed this makeshift room, I possess no more rightful claim to the hint of security and comfort it affords than he. Laws that apply to the common man are bent and twisted into strange shapes here, sometimes broken and reforged or simply left in unrecognizable pieces. And I suppose his presence provides me with something, though what that might be I can't quite say.

Is it merely desperation that draws us into these unlikely comradeships? How else to explain my affinity for a lost, haggard man with whom, though our present life circumstances are

49

not so disparate, I have so very little in common? And yet I find it enormously discouraging to accept the notion that my craving for human contact is so great that I will procure it from any source, no matter how improbable, no matter how barren, that I will see in whomever is accessible what I want or need to see to satisfy my own needs, that I'm willing to fulfill with an illusion of my own devising the yearning for a human connection and a sense of purpose. But perhaps we all do this when necessary or convenient. I'd much prefer to believe that there is something more to it, something noble and sublime. And though I know how I must sound, sneering down in hauteur at one of humankind's less fortunate offspring after enjoying a life suffused with enchantment, power, and pure delight, in my heart I know I'm in no way superior to Chick. It is only that we are, both figuratively and literally, worlds apart.

The chasm between us is far vaster than that between men of different races or cultures, or even men who haven't a single word in common. All the more inexplicable then, that we have come together, two total strangers, a fallen wizard and an inveterate tramp. My search for reasons and explanations notwithstanding, I know our meeting could have just as easily been a product of pure chance, a force to which we are all subject. Or perhaps I'm simply blind to whatever it is that we have in common. There are always things we choose not to see. Always.

CHAPTER 17

Chick

DIDN'T EVEN GET TO NO second house that night, cause the first one's where it all went to hell. We'd drove on out to this quiet area a few miles south of town, not so much what you'd call a well-to-do neighborhood, but not poor by a long shot neither. Just a nice sort of middle class–looking place in the outskirts, I guess you'd say, with two-story houses with their yards fenced in and not huddled too close together. There wasn't no traffic to speak of and it was real dark cause it's out of the city and most likely everyone who wasn't out committing crimes at that ungodly hour was home cutting z's. I was shaking and dripping sweat and no two ways about it. Truth of it is I would of given my pearly grays, each and every one, to just pack up and head on home, but I wasn't about to say nothing about it to them guys and lose face and the only friends I had at the same time. Like I say, they'd took me under their wing and kept me in pocket money and lubricated with alcohol for a goodly time. It don't make me any less guilty, but I don't think they would of taken too well to my pulling out right then and there and leaving them in the lurch. So anyways, we parked the station wagon down along a little side street and put on some gloves one of them guys'd snatched so as not to leave no fingerprints and Lenny grabbed the lug wrench and a flashlight and Phil

51

took hold of the old suitcase he brung and we went sneaking and creeping around the neighborhood, first checking out the houses from the front to make sure there was no lights on and then going from one backyard to the other until somebody someway decided what house to start on.

I guess we should of knowed right from that first slipup, when Lenny was prying open a basement window and it up and shattered on him, that we'd be best off to give it up and hightail it out of there. But Phil, he was all wide-eyed and fidgety with excitement, so when I said maybe we might want to move on to another locale just in case, I don't guess he was much listening. No, he just reaches in through the busted glass, tugs the handle on the window latch, opens it and slides hisself on in. Couldn't of been much more than a minute later, me and Lenny was slinking in the back door like a couple movie spies. I was already shaking with I guess a mix of nerves and excitement, but there wasn't nothing to do by then but stick with it. Least if there was, I sure couldn't see it.

Now, the back door was set right off of the kitchen, so after checking some drawers and only finding some beat-up odds and ends of silverware and some chipped plates and such, we went creeping into the dining room. There wasn't nothing but a regular dinner table and maybe four or five chairs in *there,* so then we proceeded on into the living room. Problem *was,* when Lenny shined his flashlight round the room we could see there wasn't hardly nothing but some big old furniture and about a couple thousand books. I ain't never seen so many books in one house in all my born days. Why, they covered every wall and went from near the floor just about up to the ceiling so there wasn't room for all them fancy doodads some folks like to show off in them big wood cases nor much of anything else. Now, there *was* this telescope-looking thing filling up one corner of the room, which for all we knowed might of been worth something, but then it's too damn big to take, and anyways, where we was going to hawk it *I* sure as hell couldn't tell you. I guess they was thinking there'd be a pile of cash and some nice suitcase-sized valuables lined up just waiting for them, or more likely they wasn't thinking nothing at all.

It was right about that time Phil and Lenny starts getting all pissed off, cause they was hoping for a big take, and plus I figure they was all agitated by whatever kind of pills they got running through their system. As for me, I just stood there, not saying nothing, sweating up my clothes pretty good and trying to keep my heart from busting out of my chest and flopping cross the floor like a buckshot rabbit. I don't know how long we was there except to say it was too goddamn long, cause I was quaking in my boots and not too particularly mindful of that sort of detail. I was mostly waiting for them two to stop pacing and decide what the hell we was going to do and hoping what we was going to do was make tracks on out of there. That's when things started to get crazy. All sudden-like Phil whips out his razor and for no reason I could see just starts going at all them books like it was *their* fault he picked the wrong damn house. For maybe a minute or so, Lenny was just holding his flashlight and watching Phil tear into them books like he's hacking his way through some jungle or such as that, but then, just when I was expecting Lenny, who was always a little calmer than Phil anyways, to step in and talk some sense into him, Lenny lifted that big old flashlight up over his head and brought it down onto the telescope with a bang you would of heard if you was stone-deaf and half a block away with your elbows jammed in your ears.

Of course it was dark again, what with the flashlight broke, and for a minute nobody was saying nothing. Right about then that room lights up and I see a pretty woman standing at the bottom of the stairs with just her nightclothes on and her skinny little finger still perched right there on the light switch. I guess she must of slipped down the steps in the dark, though I don't think none of us heard her. She didn't yell out right away neither. First, she just stares at us for a second or two, like she's trying to figure out some problem in her mind, and then she says, not loud neither, but under her breath like she was talking to her own self, "Oh my God." We was all just peering back at her when she finally turned to look upstairs and opened her mouth to holler. Stephen was the name she cried out as Phil leapt at her and grabbed a hold of her from behind.

Before I could take so much as another breath, that son of a bitch slit her throat from one side to the other like he was striking a match on the bottom of a old shoe. Then he just dropped her to the floor like a bag of garbage.

CHAPTER 18

Sam

WHEN HE FINALLY SLIPPED back in through the small makeshift door I fashioned months ago from some rusty old hinges and boards I'd liberated from a trash bin, Chick was grinning like a mischievous child. Without a word, he reached both hands deep into the pockets of that ragged overcoat he lives in, and when he brought them out he revealed several items he'd apparently purloined from some inattentive local merchant. With a smile that seemed for just a moment to strip years from that leathered face, he handed me a toothbrush, toothpaste, mouthwash, a pair of scissors, a box of tiny alcohol-infused pads, and some kind of disposable razor. "Thought you'd might find a little cleanup refreshing, so to say," he mumbled, and I could have sworn I saw a blush flare beneath his own heavy mask of dust and grime before he averted his eyes and stuttered, "Well, what I mean to say is, I thought we might could *both* do with a touch of degreasing, and maybe a little redecorating too."

Fortunately, it was already dark by the time I stepped outside and put the bristled weapon into my mouth, and now I simply haven't the heart to tell him how the blood cascaded from my tortured gums when I tried to brush the teeth that haven't already abandoned me, the searing agony I suffered with every motion of the malevolent instrument of torture. It felt as though I were chewing shards of salt-covered glass with my raw gums.

And yet it was not the sting of those odious nylon quills that nearly brought me to tears as I stood out there spitting blood. It was something else, something I couldn't quite identify.

CHAPTER 19

Chick

AS MUCH AS I WISH TO God none of that'd happened, that's only about half as much I wish that'd been the end of it. But by the time that poor lady crumbled to the floor there was already noises coming from upstairs, and it was only about a second or two later when I heard a little boy's voice whimpering for his mommy and I looked up and seen this little guy making his way downstairs, all white and trembly in his pajamas. I'll be honest, I ain't never seen nothing so horrible as that before, and the fact is I was froze up solid as a stone. I couldn't move a inch and I was hot and icy cold all at once, cause I could see clear enough his mommy's not going to answer him now or any other time.

For about a couple seconds nobody did nothing. But then there was a kind of rumble from upstairs and this man's voice hollers down to the kid to come back up and do it now. But before the little fella can even turn around, Phil latches on to his pajamas and lifts him up in front of him and holds his blade up to his throat, just like he done to the kid's mom. Well, the boy's dad hollers from upstairs to stand away from the boy or he'll fire and then he takes a step down, but I guess Phil knowed the guy wasn't going to chance hitting the little boy, cause he just steps back and says, all snarly and crazed, "You don't want to do that, Mister." But then the man says to him, "I don't believe you're stupid enough to hurt my child when he's the only thing between you and a bullet," and he keeps on coming down them steps, just as slow and steady as a funeral. The thing is, by now I'm not so sure the guy's right, and I'm about to tell him so, but my throat's closed up and I can't for the life of me get nothing out, so he keeps coming down, just dressed in his underpants and holding that big black pistol out in front of him. Now, he must not of got a good look at his wife yet, cause when he finally looks down at where she's sprawled out and sees her head just hanging there and blood spilt out all over, he lets out a howl and his knees starts to buckle and he wobbles like a sunflower in a hurricane. That's when Phil tosses the boy aside and starts to go for his old man with that godforsaken blade of his.

Fact of it is I still can't bring myself to think about what it was happened to that little boy. I guess maybe some things is better off not never getting said. Anyways, it was after the young fella got hisself killed that I finally knowed I couldn't take no more, and so I went for Phil my own self, but I was just too goddamn slow. By the time I was close enough to grab him he'd did his dirty work with his blade a second time. That kid's father just drops like a wet rag right there next to his poor wife.

I don't guess I know what we would of said anyways, but before Lenny or me could get a word out, Phil bends down and grabs the gun. He looks at me first, and then at Lenny, and then he says, "Anybody else want to fuck with me, cause I am ready." He keeps breathing hard and repeating that same thing, "I am ready," over and over until he looks up for some reason at the top of the stairs. All of a sudden he says, "How about you little girl?" Well, crouching at the top of the stairs is a little child can't be more than six years old. She's just gazing down at us like she's in some kind of trance, almost like she can't see nothing, or maybe more like she's already dead. Phil don't even pause to think or take a breath. He just turns to Lenny and says, calm and quiet, "You're going to do her, Len." After a minute goes by, Lenny looks at the floor and mumbles he don't want no part of it and asks, why him? Phil says it's cause he's the only one ain't taken part yet. Well I don't say nothing of course, cause I got nothing left, but Phil says to Lenny how I was all ready to jump into the action when the guy was going to shoot him and that means I'm okay, and a part of the killing. Lenny turns all white and glazy, but when he starts to back up Phil aims the gun at him and says, "You're going to do the girl, Len, or I'm going to do you," and then he tosses him that damn bloody blade.

I don't know exactly when it was I soiled myself, and I ain't a bit ashamed to admit to it. Fact of it is that's about the only part I *ain't* ashamed to say. Anyways, I guess Phil got a whiff of me cause he laughs and says, "If you're planning on riding with me, Sport, you'd best clean yourself up while Lenny's doing the little brat." I didn't say nothing, cause I was balled up tight as a spring and feeling all sick and twisted up tight inside. I just found the bathroom and quick as I could, cleaned myself up like he said, and when I was done I slipped out the window and hightailed it off into the woods fast as my shaky legs would take me. I fig-ure that horrible scream I heard while I was running was the last sound that poor little girl ever made. Them filthy sons of bitches killed her too.

As for me, I didn't stop running for . . . well I guess I didn't never really stop. Truth is I don't guess I'll stop till I'm finally dead and put out of my torment. Cause there ain't a single day of my miserable life I don't think on what we done to them people and how I didn't do nothing to stop it. And there ain't a day goes by I don't know just exactly what that makes me.

CHAPTER 20

Sam

I THINK IT'S BEEN A WEEK now since Chick began collecting empty bottles and cans and cashing them in at the Piggly Wiggly supermarket at the corner of Elmhurst Avenue and Twenty-Third Street. When I inquired of him what prompted this sudden alteration in his behavior, he told me that in fact it was really nothing new, explaining that on occasion he feels just compelled to earn what he called "a honest dollar." He also told me that he sometimes earns a little "pocket money" doing odd jobs, sweeping sidewalks, shoveling snow, and washing windows for some of the downtown retail businesses. I'm not certain why I assumed he knew nothing beyond cadging and petty theft. I suppose the least shameful explanation is a failure of imagination, though I cannot honestly swear there isn't something more insidious behind my disparaging surmise. I am not entirely untainted by human prejudices.

Of course, I, *too*, have found it necessary to modify certain of my ethical standards in the interest of this pale simulacrum of survival, so even if my presumptions had proved correct, it would have been both hypocritical and terribly unjust to judge my roommate's character any more harshly than I have my own. We all seem to do what we must to survive, if nothing more. At times, I wonder what it is we're hanging on to so tenaciously. Is it an attachment to this, to the minor drama we call life, or a dread of what the mysterious other might bring? Is it just another instinct designed to ensure the survival of our single-minded genes? Most likely it is some of each and then something more. Still, at times it seems a futile and pointless battle, a wearying battle for which the ultimate reward is only the ultimate failure. How strange. But maybe we reach a point, after draining all the juices from this dubious gift of life, when death, too, seems a benign bestowal.

And speaking of gifts, after more than two weeks of self-inflicted torture (he still reminds me every evening, without fail) I believe my gums might finally have wearied of spilling blood, or maybe I'm simply running low of the precious ferric fluid. In any case, the nightly crimson gusher has diminished now to a thin pinkish stream.

When he asked me, one morning early on, about a bloodstain on the gravel outside our shelter, I lied. I told him he'd slept through a violent catfight. But then he was furious with me for days for allowing such a thing to go on. Having spent the great majority of this latter lifetime alone, I am unused to having anyone to whom to answer. Sometimes, I have learned, the truth does far more harm than good, but I fear I'll need to rehearse my deceptions if we are to continue our cohabitation in peace. If a little discomfort and occasional minor deceptions are the only price I pay for his companionship, I believe I've bargained well.

But now there is something else afoot with my roommate: he has begun grilling me on occasion late at night. "So," he'll say, apparently attempting to act casual and uninterested, "ever do any other kind of work than your wizard business and such as that?"

"Well," I'll respond, "ever since the seizure that robbed me of the great preponderance of my power, I have had to make my way like any other man without a home or the other customary trappings of a profitable life."

"Okay then," he'll rejoin, after a moment of silent consideration, or a noisy clearing of his throat, "but what about before that? Didn't you never hold no regular profession of some kind?"

It is manifest in his tone, and in his cautious if clumsy approach, that he does not wish to offend me, that, in fact, he believes my true life story is other than the one I've related. But I can see no reason to lie to him about who I am or what I was. Though my honesty might bring my fellow mendicant some slight discomfort, I see no harm in challenging his illusions.

Should I invent some bland pedestrian existence to satisfy the constraints of his imagination? No. Let him struggle and squirm. Isn't that how we often learn? When we are so old that we can no longer learn, it's probably time to take our leave and make room for the next doomed fool.

CHAPTER 21

Claire

THOSE WHO ARE ACQUAINTED with the details of my story seem to find it difficult to understand why I would choose to live here again, in the same house where I was robbed of everything that mattered. Maybe *difficult* is too weak a word. I've seen people become agitated, even angry, when they learned of my decision. But those few who truly know me recognize now that I had no choice. I had to be here, in case he returned. Yes, my most horrific memories were bred in this house, but then so were my most cherished moments, and there were so many of those. And it isn't as though I could ever forget what happened, even if I lived in a cave ten thousand miles away. This wheelchair, too, binds me to that gruesome night. And I'm certainly not walking away from it.

At least I know how it is that I became the woman I am today. I don't have to wonder. I was crippled, both in body and soul, by a single, awful, unforeseeable event. Some wounds heal over time, but the scars, I've learned, are eternal. I try hard not to use them to gain sympathy or to excuse the flaws in my character, but I no longer see any point in trying to cover them up.

CHAPTER 22

Chick

SOME FOLKS MIGHT WONDER how it is I could commit any kind of crime or take another thing wasn't mine after what happened that night. And I guess I can see why they'd feel that way, but in all the years since then I never once let myself get within spitting distance of a situation where I thought there'd even be a chance to bring injury to another soul. I don't want to say I come to terms with the things I got to do to survive now, cause that ain't entirely correct neither. But like I say, a man is what he is and I just ain't made for what you might call high integrity. And I just ain't got the stomach nor the skills to fake it.

Now I suppose you could say my mom was kind of religious in her own way. Leastwise she made a whole host of god-fearing exclamations when she was angry or upset at me or my pa or some neighbor who was making a racket when she was trying to sleep off a night of hard drinking and scrapping with my pa. Plus which, she went to church almost regular and advised me sternly on the devil whenever she decided I was heading toward some infraction she figured might get me a early introduction. More often than not she'd punctuate her lessons with a smack. Course I never *did* see how all that so-called religiosity did her any good. She didn't have no kind of life to boast on, and for all her bustle about the good lord *this* and the good lord *that*, I don't see how she was any more upright than most of the godless souls I run into out here on the street. Course there's good and bad everywhere, I suppose and, if my experience is worth consideration, maybe a touch more bad than good. And there's plenty of folks what for one reason or the other just can't seem to bring themselfs above what you'd call their life situation. But I'd still say a person can't be judged just by what you see, or even by what he seems to of come to. Anyways, that's my opinion on the topic.

Now, I ain't saying I myself fit into that particular category, cause I don't figure that's the case. I'm only saying what I seen in my years of studying human nature, and I guess I'm saying too that it's this kind of thinking nags at me when I consider old Sam there. And I won't deny what that my curiosity's been roused but good. Still in all, I guess I can't pry into what's none of my affair. Plus which, from what I can see, them books has been closed for a fair period of time, and the key throwed away, too.

Least that nasty breath of his has improved some from what it was before, though it's still got quite a ways to go before you'd want to call it regular nontoxic human-type breath.

CHAPTER 23

Sam

I WISH I COULD FIND SOME sort of explanation for this growing sense of foreboding. I wish I knew what was tugging at me, dragging me down like an unrelenting undertow into the darkest depths of some turbulent sea. But it is just too distant, too vague for me to grab a hold of. And I am increasingly weary, my instincts dulled. Perhaps this is what dying feels like, or its prelude.

CHAPTER 24

Claire

MAYBE IF I COULD COMPLETELY give up hope I would find some kind of peace. But what would become of me if I relinquished my only lifeline? It may be frayed and tethered to a fading specter, but it is a lifeline nonetheless and I'm not certain I'd have the courage to remain afloat without it.

CHAPTER 25

Chick

HERE'S ONE GIVE ME A case of the shivery fits. Old Sam was going on again the other night about this guy whose mind waves he figures he's picking up on when he says he got some more details to report if I was interested. Well, I'm always willing to sit back and listen when he gets on one of his gabble-blathers, so I perk up my ears, get good and comfortable, and give him the go-ahead.

For a while there he's pretty much telling me the same kind of gobbledygook he's said before, but after a couple minutes he says how he seen this guy of his all surrounded by books and more books. Well, I close to shit my trousers on the spot. All I can think when I finally catch my breath is, either he knows what the three of us done, which just ain't possible, or he's somehow latched onto my old memories, like maybe I'm someway transmitting information about that night like some kind of goddamn human radio station. I could feel the sweat pouring off my damn forehead, and even in the dark he must of noticed it too, cause he right then leans over so close I can feel that his breath right here on my cheek, and says, "Are you growing ill, Chick?"

Now, do I think he was actually picking up on my thoughts? Well, in the cold light of day that don't seem quite so likely as it

68

did when he first mentioned them books and it was dark and creepy in here. And truth be told, I imagine there's a whole lot of folks has rooms all filled up with books and the like. Still, it put a sizable hitch in my giddyup and eat into my sleeping time by more than I'd care to admit to the persecuting attorney.

I guess a more likely circumstance is that my own ratty old brain bucket's about a quart short of oil and old Sam hisself is some kind of figment of my imagination. On the other hand, I'd truly hope if I was going to go out and conjure a figment to prey on my guilty conscience, I'd make me a better smelling one than old Sam, and while I was at it, maybe one with more feminine-like features.

Now *there's* something would more than likely clear out whatever cobwebs is tangled up in my creaky old noggin. I'm not sure I'd know what to do with a lady if I had one right here next to me, but I guess I'd be willing to try and sort it out for a little while, given the opportunity. Course, even *I'm* not so far gone I don't realize what the chances are of finding myself any feminine company in my present circumstance—leastwise any what doesn't stand on four legs and have herself a secure future on a plastic hanger in the sweater section at the Kmart. And I don't guess I'd never get that desperate.

It might be hard to believe but I *did* make the acquaintance of a couple-few ladies here and there in my travels, and too when I was younger and not quite so shoddy looking. Fact of it is, I can still remember my first full-on kiss, not that there was many others to confuse it with. Karen Shiffer her name was. We was only in the fourth grade, or maybe it was the fifth. Anyways, she set at the desk right next to mine and she was all the time talking dirty to me and sending me notes when Mrs. Palmer wasn't aiming her sizable beak our way. I don't imagine she was too clear on what it was she was saying at the time, but then neither was I. Still in all, I won't never forget the time we met after school and hid out back of the big old pine tree on Crystal Street. That snaky little tongue of hers pushed its way into my mouth and darted around in there till I thought my pants would split on open and we'd both of us be in over our head. It never did come to more than that, us being children and all, but it give me a pretty good idea what was coming my way a couple years down the road. Course, it's been so long now since I even kissed a lady I'd probably make a fool of myself and make quick work of it too. At least that's *one* problem I ain't going to have to worry about any time soon.

CHAPTER 26

Sam

EVERY DAY, IT SEEMS, I glimpse just a tiny bit more of the mystifying man who has encroached upon my vespertine ruminations. It isn't really him I see, I'm afraid, but a foggy portion of the world he inhabits. I seem to see what he is seeing, or was seeing, or will be seeing on a single day or night. Still, what began as a distant blur of distressing feelings has gradually become a mix of murky images and fleeting flashes of light, and every day they become just a little clearer, a bit more disturbingly distinct.

Weeks ago I saw for the first time a room filled with books, then, days later, a staircase appeared, and more recently I have seen a lovely young woman. She is asleep, or appears to be, and there is a flowing scarlet scarf, or maybe it's a handkerchief, draped around her neck. Unfortunately, these ephemeral glimmers recede too hastily for me to be certain of their finer features.

After his response to my last report I am somewhat reluctant to update Chick regarding my clairvoyant drama. And yet whom else do I have? Who else would care to listen? I can see no reason why these cryptic visions should cause *him* any distress. I don't ask him to pose an explanation or to offer advice; I merely want him to listen, to occasionally nod or clear his throat and purse his lips. I'm not certain why, but it is somehow more ful-

71

filling to talk to yourself when someone is in the room than it is when you know you are alone.

There is clearly something to be said for this sharing, though it is also riddled with camouflaged mines and sudden, unanticipated pitfalls. Just when you're finally convinced that you've developed the necessary skills, you find you've made yet another faux pas. And it seems there is always more to learn about those with whom you choose to pass your time—more to learn about yourself, for that matter. It is odd, though, that we might continue to grow in some ways even as we molder in so many others, odd indeed that we should learn lessons we have an ever-shrinking paucity of time or opportunity to put to use.

So let me be clear. By no means is this comradeship in which I am a partner exclusively a beneficial one. There can be . . . no, there *is*, occasionally, great frustration, and even anger. I have sacrificed my privacy, my precious silent hours, and, at times, my very comfort, or what I've begrudgingly come to think of as comfort. I have made space where there is scarcely enough for me, given an ear to his desultory ramblings when I'd rather listen to the rush of traffic, the slapping of raindrops on the stairs above, or the whistle of the moody autumn breeze as it rushes through the interstices in the slipshod structure of my . . . of our humble domicile. And my security, too, has likely been compromised by his presence. Still, except for those few moments when I am the most severely frustrated or annoyed, those moments when my temper is at its end, it seems the reward is greater, at least so far, than the cost.

On another topic, there was, in my most recent vision, a new and more disturbing element. In addition to the books and the sleeping woman with the scarlet scarf, there was a menacing presence, a man who stood holding something or someone in front of him. In the brief time I had to focus, I saw nothing to manifestly indicate it, and yet I had an overwhelming sense of impending calamity, a feeling the like of which I'd never before experienced, as though I were witnessing a train charging blindly toward a section of track to which someone lay tethered. It was an almost tangible sensation, and though the trembling and sweating have since abated, no matter how I try to shake it off, the feeling of doom has not receded.

I have found that as my obsession with this other man's life grows, my back becomes increasingly temperamental, susceptible to the slightest changes in humidity and temperature. On some days, when I waken and try to pull myself up, the process is protracted and agonizing. At times I have no choice but to remain motionless, waiting for the vice that grips my worn muscles and withered tendons to unclench just a little before attempting the torturous movement again. And there is a soreness in my neck, as though something were protruding from my throat. Perhaps I'm just coming down with the flu.

Since the decline I have been subject to a variety of aches and pains, and I've come to accept them, I suppose. Having nowhere in particular to go, there is seldom any need for me to rush off like a schoolboy, and yet this particular sort of stifling incapacity is not something for which I feel emotionally equipped. The idea of being restricted by corporeal constraints, unable to simply move about, or reliant upon another to do so, is unthinkable. It is one thing to lose the powers that elevate you above humanity, something else entirely to lose the ability to fend for yourself like any other animal. That indignity would be beyond my ken, and yet I'll have no alternative but to accept it should it continue to vex me. If I am unable to rise in the morning, or if I find I cannot twist my body around to look behind me when I hear something skittering across the floor, no amount of philosophizing will alter it. Would that it could, for I am more than capable when it comes to analyzing and philosophizing and ratiocinating. It is the acting now that seems to slow me. Damned human frailty. When I recall what I once was, realizing what I've become feels like a vicious insult hurled by the universe itself.

Before the fall I lived a hundred blessed lives in a single passing of the sun: I bestowed wisdom on my followers, fought and won battles without spilling a single precious drop of blood.

I traveled the Milky Way, a dozen dazzled children clinging to my robe, stars sifting through their hair, and I visited with kings and queens. I dallied with a sweet stunning goddess and from the flames of our passion emerged a pair of angels who watched over us and bound us even closer together. And yet, no matter how I struggle, I cannot glimpse the features of those I held so very dear. My faceless nymph, our nameless seraphs. Who were they? Where did they go when I tumbled?

CHAPTER 27

Claire

I DON'T SUPPOSE I WOULD have survived for very long if it hadn't been for my mother's dear, sweet parents, overwhelmed and emotionally undone as they were. Though it was a dismal time for all of us, and we certainly didn't always agree, I owe my sanity, my very life, to them. I was a particularly difficult child, and at times I played on their sympathy, but they always knew that I loved them as dearly as my bruised and battered heart would allow.

I guess the worst time for us, after the initial shock and those early years when we all still had a glimmer of hope that Father might someday return, was when I told them I wanted to buy this house, to live here again. Still, despite their resistance and their understandable concern for my emotional well-being, they did all they could to assist me in its acquisition. And the truth is that I've been spared some of the pain I might have felt. Who knows what I would be, what my life would be like and how I would feel if not for the psychological shock that wiped from my mind what must have been the worst of that night's images.

I can recall that horrible man plodding up the stairs after me, his expression a twisted mix of terror and psychotic rage, and I remember my stumbling flight into the bedroom, and how I struggled to bolt the door behind me, my hands trembling like tiny branches, my heart pummeling my chest as though it, too, was trying to escape. I'll never forget how I strained to force the window open, and the deafening scream that broke free as I leapt into the darkness. But I don't remember any of what I now know came before that. I only know that my mother and my brother were brutally murdered, that I was permanently crippled, and that my father's life was destroyed. And that's more than enough for me.

CHAPTER 28

Chick

SON OF A BITCH KNOWS. Simple as that. The son of a bitch somehow knows. Maybe he don't know quite what it is he knows, but I'll be damned to hell right here and now if he ain't seeing right into my terriblest recollections and spitting them out at me a creepy old sliver at a time.

For a while there I was perfectly contented just supposing there was some dumb-luck kind of coincidence in all Sam's visioning, but the other night, when he up and says he seen a flash of a blade and that there was two or maybe three other men, my old heart pretty near jumped ship. That's just too much of a coincidence for my personal discomfort.

Now, the only other thing I could come up with was maybe I'd finally blew a major brain gasket. I know I can get a little squirrelly at times, particularly when I been hitting the hard stuff extra heavy, but I ain't never had no invite to the loony bin and I ain't all that keen on the idea of trying out their particular brand of hospitality. That's why I done a sort of a test yesterday, when me and Sam was down by the courthouse getting some air and trying to pick up some pocket change.

First off, I waited till I was sure Sam wasn't paying me no mind, and then I just sidled up to a complete and total stranger and quick pointed over at old Sam and said, real quiet-like, "Hey bud, you see that old bearded guy over there?" Well for about a minute the fella gives me the once-over, like I'm a pile of horseshit and he's the King of Siam or some such thing as that. Finally, he gives me a kind of irritated-looking smirk and says, "Yeah, what of it?" Course, I had nothing to say then, cause he pretty much answered my question, so I just walked away.

Thing is, I can't for the life of me figure if this is good news or bad. I mean, if this guy hadn't of seen Sam it would of meant I was having delusions of some kind, and if he *did*, which he says he did, that would of maybe meant I got myself hooked up with some actual real-life wizard or at least a mind reader. Problem is, there ain't no such a thing as a goddamned wizard, or mind reading neither.

Course then, another possibility could be that I ain't hallucinating him at all, but I *am* hallucinating what I think he's saying. Like maybe he's sitting there blabbing about the price of tea in China and I'm hearing all that other stuff. But I got a hard time believing my weary old brain would all of a sudden conjure up such a complicated scheme as that just to punish its own self. It's done a pretty good job up till now without that kind of monkey-shines. On the other hand, if I was to say, just for the sake of argument, that I thought he *was* working some kind of voodoo mind reading on me, I'd still have to wonder why in the blue blazes he was doing it. What's the point of telling me what I already know better than anyone? That's a lot of work for no reward.

I'll be damned if I can make heads or tails of it, and truth is, it makes me all dizzy and confused just trying, not to mention sickly in my gut. The only explanation makes any sense at all don't make a single bit of sense, but I looked at this thing six ways to Sunday and there ain't one thing about it that does make sense. None of that don't change the facts, though. One way or the other, the son of a bitch knows, or my name ain't Chick.

Now hell. That don't work so good neither.

CHAPTER 29

Sam

FOR SOME REASON, my increasing obsession with the stranger in my visions appears now to be afflicting my roommate with an almost equal potency. Chick seems both frightened and intrigued by my nightly visions. I can see the odd mix of anticipation and apprehension on his face each time I speak of some new revelation. It's as though we are both being drawn toward this faceless eidolon, called upon to save him from some terrible fate.

Were I convinced he could be rescued from whatever it is that my visions presage, I would still have no clue as to where to begin. And yet he simply refuses to leave me alone. I only wish he'd chosen someone else to aid him, someone who's up to the task.

CHAPTER 30

Chick

I CAN'T FOR THE LIFE OF me figure out the whys and where-fores of it, but it seems to me like maybe Sam's someway trying to get me to go back to the scene of the crime. Thing is, it ain't clear even *he* knows he's doing it. It's more like something's making him do it, like he's got hisself hypnotized or such as that. I once seen one of them hypnotist guys get a old lady to run around the stage flapping her arms and clucking like a goddamn chicken on its way to the fry pan, which when he snapped his fingers she said she didn't know nothing about it and didn't even *eat* chicken. Anyways, I don't guess the old gasbag would try to play no nasty tricks on me if he actually knowed he was playing them. He just ain't like that.

But now he's saying he wants to try and find the guy he thinks he's been honing in on and rescue him. I guess he thinks he can someway stop it with his spells or whammies or some other sil-ly-ass shit that don't exist. He don't know it's already happened and the poor guy is dead, and unless I been gabbing in my sleep, he don't know I was right there in the middle of it when it did happen.

So what am I supposed to do? I don't believe in no supernat-ural spirit world or mind reading or much of anything else, but it seems to me like somebody or the other's trying awful damn hard to get me to go back to that godforsaken place. With all of this reminding, this place don't feel so homey no more and it might be that some kind of change would be good for Sam, even if it was just to get his creaky old limbs moving around and his mind off this stuff. I don't like the idea one bit, but maybe I ought to just go ahead back and take a good long gander at that damn house and take him right along with me and get it out of everybody's system once and for all. I ain't been anywheres near that damn place since that night, and I ain't never figured on *going* back, but who knows, maybe it'd do me some kind of good to go there in person and face up to it. Or maybe it'd finally kill me, which I figure would be okay too and would sure as shit put a quick end to all this worrying and figuring.

True fact of it is I don't know *what* makes sense no more, and I guess maybe I never did. Could be it's time we take us a little trip and be done with it. Neither one of us has got one hell of a lot to lose and just being in motion might be good for us. Now, how I'm supposed to tell Sam I think I can find the place he's looking for I do not know, but I imagine I could come up with some kind of bullshit or the other. That's something I figure I've got pretty good at.

CHAPTER 31

Claire

SURELY MUCH OF THE DEPRESSION I suffered growing up was a result of the unresolved anger and resentment I felt toward my father for abandoning me, and maybe for not protecting me, for not protecting us all. I understand now, and I suppose some part of me always has, that losing his sanity was not a conscious choice. I know too, because I know him, and because I've read and reread the police reports, that he must have done all he could have done that night to save his wife and children. What kind of man could go through what he did, what kind of man could watch as his loved ones were slaughtered, and survive unscathed? Losing his mind, his memory, his identity may well have been far better for him than enduring what he would have had to endure had he known when he awoke what had happened and who he was. And I don't see how he could have abdicated his own identity without tearing himself from me. To him I was just a stranger in a hospital room, a sad little girl lying half-paralyzed, barely half-conscious next to a man who'd lost his reason to live, to be who he was. I still believe he would have recognized me if there was any way he could have done so without gutting his own soul. But then I need to believe that.

And yet I, who had just lost a brother and a mother, not to mention the use of my legs, was now left without a father, too. Of course there is very little common ground between logic and emotion. What I felt for that scarred and broken man who disappeared from the hospital in the middle of the night and never returned was an uncomfortable mixture of deep love and bitter indignation. How could you abandon me when I need you the most? It may be that what I feel now, today, is just an aged and ripened version of what I was feeling then. Even the strongest emotions can be slippery and elusive when one tries to grab ahold of them.

I suppose, after a certain point, after we reach a particular age or after we've been formed by whatever the elements and events are that conspire to whittle us into what we ultimately become, we aren't likely to change all that much. We settle and harden like cooling lava. We become something solid and immutable, with crags and hollows inside and out. And then, when fortune finally smiles upon us, we cease to be. Only then does the suffering end.

CHAPTER 32

Sam

THIS MAN I'VE TAKEN AS A friend and companion is an increasingly fascinating creature. His eagerness to assist me in my newfound quest is touching, if somewhat baffling, and his suggestion regarding how we might locate the man in my visions, however farfetched, however illogical, reveals a sort of creativity I would never have expected to find in one such as him. *One such as him.* But who and what is he? There is a question worth pondering, had I centuries more during which to do it. His plan, as I understand it, is for me to attempt to gain a stronger sense, a clearer image of the house, the surroundings, and the neighborhood, and then to describe to him in great detail everything I can. He tells me he's traveled around this country so much that he might, just by hearing my description, be able to help me locate the neighborhood, even the very house in my visions. Additionally, he has hinted that he's begun to have what he describes as his own "psychotic visionings." I can't help but laugh, of course, not only at his choice of words, but at the idea that he might have the means to deliver me to this man. But then I would do well to remember how ludicrous my own story must sound to him, and to the few others with whom I've deigned to share it. As unlikely as it seems, there may be more to him than at first blush it appeared. We shall see.

Yes, in my most logical, lucid moments I know there is nothing he or anyone else can do, but I have no reason to stay here or, for that matter, any other earthly place. Perhaps some motion and a sense of purpose, however false, would do me some good. And isn't it hope, that pretty lie, that seduces us and keeps us going? Don't we all survive through illusions and subterfuge, fantasies of a greater purpose, a concrete truth, a lasting legacy, some form of immortality? Where is the harm in hoping when losing hope is like death, but without the welcome silence?

CHAPTER 33

Chick

NOW WHO'S TRICKING WHO? That's what I want to know. Sure as shit stinks when it's fresh and steamy, I got a screw loose, and a critical one at that. Here I got this make-believe wizard reading my mind about some poor dead guy and scaring the shit out of me to boot, and what do I do? I'll tell you what I do. I for some goddamn reason make up my mind I got to go back to where all that horrible stuff happened and face up to my old demons. Then what do I do? I tell Sam he's been blabbing in his sleep every night about someplace called Scranton and describing a house and a neighborhood and all. And I tell him that's a town in Pennsylvania and from his sleep talking I think I can maybe find where this guy he thinks he can save might be residing. Christ almighty in a outhouse.

I guess if I was really going to be a good friend I'd just up and confess to him and save him the considerable might and mane it's going to take us to go all the way to Scranton to find a guy who ain't there. It might be good to finally tell somebody what I done and just get it off my chest, or at least give it a try, but you don't make a whole lot of friends living the way I do, and I've for some reason grown mightily fond of old Sam. I guess I'm fonder of him than I been of anyone I can recall knowing and I wouldn't care to

86

find out what he'd think of me if he knew what I done. I already figured out there ain't no God up there pulling strings and running the show, but I like to think maybe there's some reason or the other why we two come together, and maybe there's some reason for me to go ahead back to Scranton, even if it's just to die and end this foolishness. Course it's more than I can get a grasp on, but then so is a fair majority of what I've seen in my life. And I sure as hell got nothing holding me here in Muncie—nothing but empty pockets and a belly full of gas, that is.

Only real problem is how we're going to get from here to there, and I guess I can someway figure that one out if I set my mind onto it, or what's left of it anyways.

CHAPTER 34

Sam

CLEARLY, THERE IS NO LOGIC to it, and maybe it is nothing more than illusion, a mischievous ruse devised by an evanescent mind, and yet when he pronounced the name of that Pennsylvania city my throat contracted and a chill spread throughout my weary body. It was as though someone were infusing ice water into the chambers of my heart. Surely it isn't the poetry of the word. To my ear, at least, Scranton is a singularly harsh and distasteful appellation.

Perhaps I am deceiving myself, but in spite of the glaring illogic of the idea, it's possible that I was drawn to Chick because he knows this city I've been divulging in my sleep. That may be the reason I felt compelled to offer him shelter and friendship. Without the awareness that I was doing it, I may have unearthed the man who can lead me to the one who is calling out for help. If there's another explanation, I don't see it.

So if Chick is willing, which it seems he is, we will travel together to find the man who inhabits the scenes I've been witnessing, or, for all I know, to learn that no such man exists. If it isn't already too late, we will do all we can to forestall his fate. Indeed, I do have a renewed sense of hope, for if there were nothing for me to do, why would I suffer the visions at all? What purpose would they serve other than to upset me, and why would I have found Chick? After so many years of idle wandering, perhaps I have found a new purpose, something of value to hold on to. It can't be too much to ask, just to matter.

CHAPTER 35

Claire

PERHAPS THINGS WOULD have been easier if I'd been able to face the men who destroyed our lives, to scream at them until my voice shattered, to beat them until the bones in my fists splintered, to see them punished in ways I'm not barbarous enough to imagine. Maybe if there had been someone tangible to blame, someone at whom to direct my rage; maybe if there'd been a trial, a conviction, and a harsh, merciless sentence, I would have found it possible to move on.

As it is, I know that two men, two desperate derelicts, were chased down and trapped by the police only hours after the slaughter, and that when the men tried to shoot their way out, the police returned their fire and killed them both. I know too that the motive was robbery and that there may or may not have been a third man. At times I think I recall a third, but I have no reason to trust any of those distant recollections. Most of the time all I can remember is my brief flight. And anyway, who listens to a traumatized child?

I know that the men were trying to rob our house when my mother stumbled upon them and that my mother was probably already dead when my father came down. I know that I, too, would be dead if I hadn't run and leapt from the window. Why in God's name they shot Timmy, and how they got my father's gun, is unclear . . . and unimportant, I suppose. Nothing they did makes sense to me and no reason would make sense to me.

Would I feel better if I could have asked those men how they chose our house, why they didn't just run when my mother caught them? Would my life really be different, better, if I could have exacted some sort of violent vengeance, if I could have watched them suffer and die? I'll never know, and I'm not at all certain I'd want to know the answers now.

Still, it requires a special talent and some extra effort to hate the dead, to loathe the mere thought of someone who no longer exists. But then I've had years to hone the skill.

CHAPTER 36

Chick

WELL I'LL BE A SAGGY-ASS SON of a bitch if old Sam isn't all of a sudden anxiouser than a starving field mouse in a cheddar cheese factory. No sooner do I mention the city of Scranton by name than he's packing up his toothbrush and getting ready to pull up stakes. You would of thought I had us a couple first class tickets to the Bermuda shorts. I had to calm him down and remind him we got no car and no money to speak of and consequently no damn way to get where we think we want to go but probably shouldn't anyways. He's all energized and ready to rush out and hardly listening to the finer details of the situation until I finally grab him by them bony shoulders and say, "Unless you're planning on zapping us there on your magical carpet, we still got ourselfs something of a problem." That's when he looks at me and says, all dark and serious-like, "I guess I still haven't fully adjusted to the corporal limitations of morality," or some such flapdoodle.

That was more than three weeks ago and I'll be damned if he hasn't up and got busier than a whole hive of honeybees in heat since then. Why, he's out collecting cans all damn night and running around who-knows-where all day. Anyways, somehow or the other he's already saved up near a hundred-seventy dollars for the trip. When you add in the forty-some dollars I got stashed in my good shoe, I figure we must be getting pretty close to a couple of Greyhound tickets to Pennsylvania, one-way, leastwise, and seeing as I don't feel no particular compulsion to return back here to Muncie, and seeing as I don't guess he does neither, we'll just worry about that circumstance when and if we smash into it. When you live out here on the street, it don't much matter what town you're in. One place is pretty much the same as the other far as I can tell, and I figure I been around more than most. Sure, some places maybe got nicer weather than others, and some's got cops or thugs, which is pretty much the same thing, with nothing better to do with their time than roust some poor beggar from a park bench or a bus station so the rats can have it to theirselves, but still in all, you figure out what's what soon enough if you want to keep breathing, which maybe sometimes you do and maybe sometimes you don't. You find your place and try and make it feel like home, even though you know good and well it don't come close. I guess you someway know that even if you ain't never had a home.

I ain't no expert, but it seems to me home's a variable concept anyways. If things is good and you got a house and family, you might maybe wish you had a bigger house or a nicer yard, but when you ain't had nothing for thirty years or so your biggest hope is you won't drown or freeze to death or get eaten by some kind of nasty vermin while you sleep off a bad drunk you got from borrowed rotgut. I guess what's important to you on any number of subjects depends on what you got at the time. If you're starving, maybe all you want's some food, and it don't matter much if it tastes like it got scraped off a tractor tire, which it most probably did. If you're freezing, there maybe ain't nothing on your mind except finding some way or the other to stop the shivering and getting the feeling back in your hands and feet. Course then, there's times when being numb's a gift and you regret getting the pain back. I suppose if you was lonely enough, you'd maybe find yourself some make-believe company, kind of like I for a while thought I might be doing with old Sam. If things is bad enough, you get to the point where you're just a wild animal and you can't think much past whatever it is you need but ain't got at that very minute. And I don't suppose there's much a person won't do if he's desperate enough or selfish enough or cruel enough.

Fact of it is I could maybe live a little better with myself if I could someway trick myself into thinking we for some reason had to do what we done to that poor family. Like if it was them or us, or even if we was crazed with hunger and maybe out of our mind. But that just ain't the case. We all three of us had a choice. That woman sure as hell wasn't going to do us no harm standing there in her nightgown about to faint from fear.

I guess you might think I would of put that behind me a long time ago, and, truth to be told, I've had some extended periods where I didn't much think about it, but eventually it'll come back and remind me of who I am with a good hard slap in the conscience, so to say. Maybe there's some could let it go entirely, chalk it up to being young and all, and maybe they're better off than me, but they ain't me, and I ain't so sure I'd care to be them in spite of their comfort. I don't take no particular pleasure in my guiltiness, but then I wouldn't like to think what I'd be without it neither.

CHAPTER 37

Sam

THERE IS SOMETHING bittersweet in the changes that have been taking place. There is an enlivening sense of control, or at least the illusion of control, in taking action again, in performing an honest day's work, whether it is collecting cans, cleaning windows, or unloading a truck bursting with fresh produce. Furthermore, my sense of purpose, so long absent, has been revived in these last few weeks. And yet, attached to all of that is an amorphous discomfort, like a distant echo, a reminder of something I cannot quite evoke, like the awful feeling that remains after all the details of a terrible dream have faded.

But why should it be that in beginning to act more responsibly, in taking control of my life again rather than continuing to flounder aimlessly about, I have triggered this shapeless portent? It isn't as though I've never before held a job. Over the course of these declining years I've labored in a great variety of menial trades. Of course my objective in the past was mere subsistence: food, shelter, drink—the most basic comforts and little more. There was no commitment, no purpose beyond satisfying those immediate needs. Now I'm working toward a greater goal, or at least it seems so to me. Now I go out every morning to work, or to search for work, and every night when my work or my search is completed, I return to the same place, to my home, where, waiting for me, is my friend, my partner in this peculiar and unexpected life journey.

Isn't it interesting, though, that now that I have a mission, now that I can see a path and have some sort of a home to come back to, I would choose to uproot myself? But perhaps the path chose me. It doesn't matter, for here we are, and as sure as I was once a venerable and potent wizard, this was meant to be. And in spite of my trepidation I am growing impatient now.

CHAPTER 38

Chick

JUST WHEN YOU THINK YOU got everything pretty near worked out, you come to find out it ain't going to be quite so smooth as you might of figured. First off, there ain't no direct bus from Muncie to Scranton. Hell no. That'd be too damn easy. Instead, you gotta take a bus from Muncie to Indianapolis and then you gotta stay overnight somewheres in Indianapolis, cause even if you get the first bus out of Muncie you just missed the last bus from Indianapolis to Scranton today cause that's how they figured to schedule it for your own personal inconvenience. Next day, if you can get yourself a ticket, you take another bus, which takes you from Indianapolis to Scranton by way of East Buttfuck or some other town you won't find on no self-respecting road map. Course that's all assuming you don't get yourself forcibly evicted from the Muncie bus station about a couple dozen times before you even get the chance to explain you ain't just there to get out of the cold rain what's been coming down in buckets for near a week now and what makes you appear even more bedraggled and pitiful than you would if you was just dry and dusty like normal, but that you want to pay American cash money for a couple of goddamn one-way tickets out of this shit-hole town. And it ain't like the folks I seen getting on and off buses while I was trying to get our tickets was the most upright looking or well-groomed bunch I ever seen neither. Fact is, for the most part they looked like they wasn't more than a couple dollars from total destitution their own selves, not that I'm casting inspersions on them. It's just that I couldn't see a whole world of difference between me and them from where *I* was standing, which, like I say, was mostly out in the cold goddamn rain.

Anyways, by the time I got the nasty old skin-sack behind the ticket window at the ABC Coachlines to finally pay me some serious mind by waving my wad of cash in her double-wide mug, my innards was rumbling something fierce. Now, for some reason I can't figure and don't necessarily want to know I ain't taken a dump for near a week. I mean it's like somebody tied a knot just north of my butthole while I was sleeping and threw away the key. Couple days ago I was pushing so hard I thought I'd broke a blood vessel in my left eye. I swear if I would of pushed any harder the top of my head would of popped off and there would of been shit and whatever brains I got splattered from here to kingdom come. So anyways, there I am, finally at the ticket booth, and all of a sudden I feel the first promising rumblings I've felt in days. "Gimme a couple of them one-way tickets to Indianapolis, please," I grunt, and I squeeze my legs together tight as I can without toppling over. Anyways, this old bag must be hard of hearing I guess, cause she leans in toward the little window hole thing and her eyebrows slides up to the top of her forehead and she says, "Excuse me?" Well, now I can feel this giant ball of lead drop down to my shit-chute and start pushing and shoving to get out right now or else. "Two tickets to Indianapolis, please," I say. "When would you like to leave, Sir?" she asks, though she kind of sneers when she says "Sir." "Day after tomorrow," I go, and now I'm sweating like a cold keg at a August picnic and shivering all at the same time. I figure we're about done when she says, "What time would you like to leave?" Well by this time there's a line of people behind me, and they's all grumbly and flustrated cause I'm taking so damn long, and while I don't blame them one bit, I'm a little too caught up in my own personal predicament to worry too much if they make their bus or not, cause I'm about to shit my only pants big-time and ruin everyone's afternoon, not to mention probably get throwed out of the damn bus station for about the hundredth time today. And I don't figure they'd be likely to invite me back any time soon after a incident of that particular nature.

So anyways, I finally get her to sell me the tickets for the first part of the ride, though once I got them in my hand she right away proceeds to tell she can't help me with the ones what'll get us from Indianapolis to Scranton cause the ABC Coachlines ain't exactly connected to Greyhound or some other diddly-ass shit. Leastwise, she *does* give me the price for them other tickets, which I appreciate, since I wasn't so sure about the price I got on the phone the other day from some customer service guy just about bit my head off in some other language for wanting some actual customer service. Must be something in the fumes gets all them bus employees so pissed off, cause I ain't spoke to a one of them yet didn't have a sizeable rodent chewing up their ass. Problem is, by the time I left the bus station my sense of emergency had taken a hike, which was more than a little disappointing, seeing how my gut feels like it's about ready to burst like a dropped pumpkin. I guess that delay right at my time of need must of somehow forced it back up wherever it's been hiding out. That's when I figured I better take some kind of action on this situation so I don't end up some night just up and exploding in my sleep and killing old Sam and maybe wiping out the church in the process.

Now, most of the time when I go into a store, I do my work quick as I can and head out before they know what's what. I also like to spread out the goodwill and not do my shopping, so to say, all at one place. That way they might not get wise to me so quick, and plus which I'd hate like hell to have one of these guys out of business just cause of my bad habits. But this time I went right back to the place where I got Sam's tooth-cleaning supplies and went on a actual shopping spree. It somehow turned out we had more money than we needed for both of them bus rides, so

I figured to get us some soap and such so as to get the smell of Muncie off us and while I'm at it pick up a box of Ex-Lax. I mean enough's enough.

Good thing I decided to pay this time too, cause I think the guy behind the counter remembered me from last time. He pretty much kept his eyes on me the whole time I was walking around. I was feeling guilty even though I wasn't doing nothing wrong. Anyways, when I got up to the register I noticed the funny look the guy had plastered on his face. First off he goes, "You actually planning to pay today?" I figured it was in my best interests to remain moot, so to say, so I just set my stuff on the counter, took out some bills, and put on a confused expression, best I could. Then he looks at my stuff and says, "Got a big night planned, don't you?" Thing is, he's sort of smiling at me now. For a minute I can't figure out what he's getting at, but then I take another look at what I'm buying: a box of extra-strength Ex-Lax, two giant-sized rolls of paper towels, a pack of sponges, and a couple bars of Ivory soap. Well, I hand him a twenty and look right at him and say, "I guess you could say I'm a optimist." We both have a good laugh at that one, and so does the young fella who's been waiting behind me.

I can't rightly say as I know why, but when I walked out of there I was feeling kind of good. Problem is, when you get a nice feeling about somebody like that, it makes it real hard to go back and take further liberties.

CHAPTER 39

Sam

I CAN SCARCELY CONCEIVE HOW I managed to survive for so long without some clear objective. It's no wonder that I've been so disheartened. Although this is very different from the days when the only limitations I could expect to encounter were those of my own imagination, I find myself reenergized by the knowledge that I have a mission, and by the prospect of a journey. Yes, there is still a sense of foreboding, but I feel alive again, and that is worth worlds to this moldering mass of meat. I'd nearly come to accept that any significance I could lay claim to was in the distant past, but now I have hope for the future, and who can say that there aren't other rewards ahead, that in this life, or in the eternal one that follows, I won't find the kind of fulfillment I can only vaguely recall? I can't remember when I've felt so hopeful. I may be courting disappointment, but for the nonce I'll take succor in this long-forgotten feeling, for it enlivens me.

As for my roommate, he seems to take enormous pleasure in managing the details of our impending voyage. And he's done better by far than ever I would have expected. If all goes as planned, we shall spend tomorrow cleaning up, and the following day we'll bid farewell to this makeshift room, this tiny rectangle that's nearly become a home. With yet another winter dispatching its blistering winds, I fear we may miss these ragged walls more than we now realize. The shelter they provide is imperfect, but it is shelter nonetheless, and I doubt we'll have the good fortune to find its like again. But then no one knows what lies ahead. Surely not this declining wizard.

CHAPTER 40

Claire

PERHAPS, HAD WE FOUND him soon after his disappearance, we could have somehow nursed him back to health. Maybe then I could have reclaimed my father and he could have rebuilt some sort of life for himself. Although those hopes faded long ago, if I knew he was alive and not in terrible pain it might be enough, or nearly enough, to satisfy me.

Sure, I have my own life now, my own routine; I have my teaching, my books, and my students; I have my rituals, and although I sometimes feel lonely or afraid, my story is mostly one of survival. I no longer wonder why I'm so troubled. What amazes me in my better moments now is how relatively well I've done. But even an adequate life somehow reclaimed from the rubble can't take away the sting of the past. That's something that will always be a part of me. Only death, I suspect, will bring me peace now. A hollow solace but it will have to suffice.

CHAPTER 41

Chick

I'M AFRAID I GOT OLD Sam's hopes up a mite more than I figured to, and to tell you the God's honest truth, I feel like a pile of shit. Thing is, he seems a touch happier now than before, and I don't guess I'd want to take that away from him. But it plagues me no end what's going to happen when we get to Scranton and there's nobody to save but a dead man and his dead family. Seems like I can't do nothing without someway fucking it up. Course that ain't no news flash but it still tears at me like a ragged-edged knife.

CHAPTER 42

Sam

IT ISN'T AS THOUGH I'VE completely neglected my hygiene throughout these past years. Though it has not always been easy, I have done my best to keep my aging body as clean as circumstances would permit. At least I thought I had. And yet, judging from the thick brown river of sludge Chick and I scoured from my red and irritated flesh, it appears that my standards are no longer what they once were. I wish it were an exaggeration, but the shameful truth is that it took more than an hour for the water that swirled into the shower drain to finally lose its deep caramel tinge and begin to become transparent. Now, every inch of my skin is tender and raw, but once the redness fades, if it ever does, I believe my natural color, whatever that might turn out to be, will have been restored.

But if my flesh was a quagmire of grime, my beard was worse. We might have furnished a small museum with the gallimaufry of odds and ends that fell from that abundant thicket of gray curls. Chick would have had me shave it off, and I fear we nearly came to blows in debating the issue, but in the end he acceded to my wish to preserve it, but only asked that I consider a minor trim at some time in the near future. I feel my beard offers me some critical protection, though I can't quite say from what.

And still my ragged orphan continues to surprise me. In fact he is proving far more useful, far more competent and industrious than ever I might have dared to imagine. When initially he raised the issue of a bath or a shower, I was certain we would be compelled to steal into some grimy gas station restroom and scrub ourselves at the sink as best we could before slipping back into the same foul garments we'd been wearing for countless months. But with a small bribe to a man whose smirk betrayed a prurient fascination with whatever sordid deeds he imagined we might be planning, Chick was able to secure for us a full three hours in a motel room. And when we were both well cleansed we attired ourselves in the vestments he'd procured for us from the Salvation Army. Notwithstanding my earlier doubts, he seems quite capable when it comes to practical issues, particularly when an understanding of the darker side of human nature is required, though that doesn't undermine my conviction that he is, at heart, a good and decent man.

What remains a mystery to me is the question of what it is that drives him. It is clear enough why I must go to Scranton; what is still not quite so clear is why Chick is equally committed to this journey. What possible gain could there be for a man whose only aspirations, as far as I can tell, are survival, some modicum of comfort, and occasional inebriation? What can there be for a homeless indigent in Scranton, Pennsylvania, that cannot be found right here in Muncie, Indiana? And aren't all mortals ultimately motivated by their own needs and desires?

"Do you have friends there?" I've asked him more than once. "I most assuredly do not," he responds, and turns his face toward the ground as though offended. "Relatives?" I inquire. "Not what I know of," he mumbles, shuffling his feet now like a child. "Money in the bank, or possibly some valuable property?" I continue, knowing what the answer must be, just playing with him now. And he only blushes. A couple days ago, when I was abusing him with my questions, he told me that he was excited by the prospect of helping a "real-life wizard." But of course that's not the answer. I suppose it's his business, and it certainly serves me well, but still, I can't help but wonder.

Whatever the explanation, we are on our way. Somehow, between us we earned more money than the trip will require, so this morning, before boarding this first bus, we actually purchased fresh food for the ride. I guess we'd forgotten about eating for these past few days, because before leaving the station we'd ravened the sandwiches originally earmarked for much later in the ride. Twenty minutes later we were both queasy, an inevitable consequence, I suppose, of gluttony, but preferable to the gnawing ache of hunger if only because it's a change from what we've come to know.

Unfortunately for all, Chick spent a great deal of the journey in the bathroom, noisily polluting the atmosphere for miles around, eventually eclipsing even the noxious fumes of the bus. If we had bathed in hopes of lessening the potential discomfort of our fellow travelers, it was all for naught. Suffice it to say we are making no new friends on this ride, and perhaps we've found a fresh enemy or two. But what is even more discouraging is the knowledge that we may find it necessary to incinerate his new trousers in order to put them out of their misery and make our corner of the planet safe again for human habitation. Ha! Now even I am making jokes.

CHAPTER 43

Chick

I'M AFRAID I MUST OF miscalculated some on just when to take them damn Ex-Lax pills for the intesticle problem I was experiencing before we headed out. I didn't figure on having quite such a severe attack as what I had, and I didn't figure on having it right there on the damn bus neither. I was up and down more than a kid's jack-in-the-box toy on Christmas Day. Things is more or less back to normal now, least as far as my inwards go. But it was a rough ride, and I wouldn't want to go through nothing like that anytime soon if I could avoid it.

Now you can slap my face and call me apple brown Betty if Indianapolis ain't every bit as much a eyesore as Muncie was, only a damn sight more frantic, so to say. And it got colder than a witch's teat and clouded up some too while we was suffering on that rickety old bus. Truth is, right about now I wouldn't mind one bit sitting back under them drafty old church steps sipping a bottle of backwash and listening to Sam blab about the rings of Uranus or the battle of arm a getting. And we got from now until tomorrow afternoon at three thirty in the p.m. to loiter around this town. Still in all, cold and tired as I am, I ain't about to piddle away the few extra bucks we got left on some fancy hotel room. No sir. We're just going to have to do what we been doing for years and find ourself someplace to lay our heads and keep warm as we can till then.

Now I ain't going to deny it, I'm more than a little bit nervous about going back to that neighborhood. I don't guess there's no reason to worry somebody's going to recognize me and whisk me off to the local jail. But I got a feeling just seeing that house is going to send a shiver through me like I ain't felt since that poor lady's throat opened up and her life seeped out onto the floor. Truth of it is I've changed my mind at least a dozen times in the last couple hours, but I don't guess I got much choice now and maybe that's for the best. I might just as well face up to it and see what it's like to not be a fully-fledged coward for once in my life. Whatever happens to me, it ain't even going to come close to what any one of them folks went through. I ain't going to get teary-eyed now, but I will say I'd give just about anything I got, not to say I got anything anybody would want, but whatever I got, I'd give it a thousand times over and more to be able to take back just one of their innocent lifes. Course that ain't going to happen, and I know it good and well. What's going to happen is I'm going to feel as bad as I felt in the last thirty-whatever years and old Sam's going to find out there ain't no one left to save and then I don't guess either one of us is going to feel much like hanging around town for the happy holidays.

I would hate like hell to lose the hairy old sack of bones as a friend and companion. And truth is I figure he's probably better off having someone around who's not quite as loony as he is to make sure he don't get hisself in too serious of a predicament. Damn it all to hell, I become awful fond of him despite of his considerable drawbacks, not the least of which is his disordered way of thinking. Still in all, I don't figure he and I's going to have much of a future together after this little trip is over.

CHAPTER 44

Claire

TODAY, WHILE ANOTHER teacher substituted for me, I substituted for a colleague who teaches a class of fourth-graders. They've been studying electricity, and as I was explaining to them some of the ways electrical currents are created, I remembered one of the experiments my father used to perform for us at home. Using a lemon or a lime, two screws, one brass and one iron, and a short length of wire, he would generate enough of an electrical charge to make a Christmas tree light glow. No matter how often he did it, we were captivated by the fact that he was drawing electricity from a piece of citrus fruit. As with the night sky and his old telescope, I think it was his own childlike fascination that drew us in so completely and captured our imaginations. Though he was a scholar, my father never lost his own childlike sense of awe.

CHAPTER 45

Sam

IT WAS BITTER COLD, and we had finally fallen asleep, huddled close together in the doorway of a burned-out liquor store, just a few blocks from the bus station. I don't know for how long I'd been slumbering when I felt the sting of the first blow, but the force of the bat against my stomach stole the wind from my lungs and made me sick and dizzy. Throughout all of the commotion, Chick was yelling to me, but not until after a second clout, this one to my jaw, did I hear his words. And it was only after spitting out a pair of bloody teeth that I was able to process their meaning.

"Curl yourself up in a ball," he repeated, while attempting to fend off an unremitting frenzy of blows to himself. I fear what might have become of us had he not somehow liberated a bat from one of the perpetrators and begun swinging it wildly over his head. He tore two of the offenders from me before all but one ran off. Chick grabbed the remaining youngster, who had tripped on something as he attempted to flee, by the collar of his jacket, and brought the bat up into the air above him again. For a terrifying moment I was certain he would bring it down on the young ruffian's head. From what I could see of the child's expression, he was far less afraid than I, but just when I was about to call out to Chick to spare the misguided lad, Chick looked over at me, his

111

eyes wild with rage. A silent second passed before he released his prey and without a word dropped the wooden weapon to the ground. "I just can't," was all he said when finally he slumped back to the sidewalk. And then he hung his head and buried his face in his hands. I stood for a moment before moving toward him, but when I put my hand on his shoulder, he just said, "No," and pushed it away like something poisonous.

The indignity was far more difficult for me to bear than was the physical pain, to be attacked and terrorized while we struggled to steal just a couple hours of sleep, and I, powerless and frightened, cowering in a dark corner like a crippled dog. Oh, how it pains me to think of what's become of me that I should suffer such a brutal drubbing at the hands of a squadron of earthborn children. What in God's name did they imagine we might possess, two frozen tramps without a roof of our own or a decent overcoat between us? And if they did it just for sport, then why choose to torture two sleeping souls whose every morning promises fresh torture? Where is the sport in that? And more baffling than all of that, how could ones so young and callow have found the time and accumulated the life experience required to become so barbaric? Who teaches them? Is it in all of us, waiting for the proper trigger to set it off? In the darkness it was difficult to distinguish the finer details of their faces, but their voices were not those of men and the one Chick was able to detain seemed barely old enough to sprout more than the faintest shadow of a downy mustache.

Suffice it to say we slept no more, and we spoke no more about the events that had transpired, though I learned, when the gray light of morning filtered through the dark distended clouds, that Chick too had been injured. A crusty stream of blood had left its path from his nose to his chin and onto his new clothes. And two of the fingers on his right hand were badly swollen and apparently stiff, though he didn't complain. I suppose we should be grateful for the numbing cold, but it doesn't come natural to one who's spent as many nights bewailing it as have I, to think of the winter's chilling bite as an ally.

And after all that has come to pass in the last twenty-four hours, I had nearly forgotten, and would that I had, for it seems clear now what I've been witnessing in my recent visions. Though it is too terrible to be true, the child's face disintegrates as he nears the man, and the poor child falls to the ground. How much more horror can be in store for the tortured soul who must stand watching this carnage, unable or unwilling, for some reason, to stop it?

CHAPTER 46

Chick

ALL I'M GOING TO SAY is it was a damn ugly night, and no two ways about it. Sometimes it seems there ain't no right and wrong, no way out but the wrong way, but I ain't none too proud of my behavior, or by what I come a little too close to doing to the one I grabbed ahold of. Other than that, I'd prefer not to speak of the matter in any specific sort of way.

Now, I guess I could of come out of the altercation a touch worse than I done, with only a couple bruises and sprains and whatnot, but I got a feeling Sam's hurt worse than he's saying, or maybe worse than he even knows. His face and jaw looks to be swole up pretty bad under that scraggly damn beard of his, and I'm guessing he's going to be eating a strict diet of soup for the next little while. Course, when I suggested that we maybe ought to get him to the nearest hospital he got all persnickety and wouldn't have none of it. Anyways, I wish I could at least see how bad he's hurt, but he ain't about to let me root around in that forest of hair, and I suppose it might be just as well. No telling what kind of wildlife I'd might still find scurrying around in the underbrush. Like to lose a finger right up to my shoulder if I wasn't careful.

Anyways, way it all turned out, we limped onto the bus right at three thirty, and after about a half a dozen stops, even *with* all the snow and the slippery roads and such, we was only just ten minutes late, pulling into the Pittsburgh bus terminal at one thirty in the morning. Problem is, now that they're pretty near ready to head on out again, it's coming down out there like grated cheese on a giant bowl of spaghetti. They ain't sure if they're going to keep on going now or wait till it's done mussing up the highway to go on ahead. The way I got it figured, the longer they hold off, the deeper the snow's going to get, but I don't guess anybody's going to be soliciting my opinions on that subject or any other anytime soon.

It don't matter where you are, people just treat you different when you look like a bum. Even scrubbed up and without the extra decorating them kids did on us, I guess we didn't look like the most savory individuals you'd ever hope to meet. I suppose the destitution is what you might call "ground in," kind of like the dirt was before we got all scrubbed up. Seems to me when you lose your hope you also lose some of your natural shimmer. I myself seen a whole shitload of blank faces and empty eyes out there on the street, though I seen that same expression on the faces of more than a few working folks too. I guess a person could have just about everything and still lose hope.

Course now that we're all beat up most of the people on this new bus just does their best to ignore us, leastwise when they think we might could see them. I figure we give them some peculiar kind of entertainment or something when they think they can sneak a glance without getting caught. But then I also figure they're a little ashamed, or maybe afraid, though I'm not sure neither one of us could muster the energy to do any serious harm even if we did want to.

Truth to be told, it takes all I got just to get through the day. I sure as shit don't need to make it worse by going out of my way and trying to get in trouble with the other citizens. Sure, I might ask for some help from a passerby on occasion, or take a little bit of what's not mine when nobody's looking, but I got no interest in any kind of confrontation and I sure wouldn't care to do no more damage than what I already done. Probably the only reason I ain't living in constant fear my *own* self is I don't care all that much about anything I got to lose. When all you got to eat's a moldy old piece of bread or another goddamn cold hamburger, you don't do a lot of wailing if somebody bigger or meaner up and grabs it from you. Help yourself. It's likely got a pretty foul taste anyway, and it sure as shit ain't going to satisfy your hunger none. The only other thing I got to lose is my life, and ain't nobody putting a lot of value on that. Now, I'm not saying I especially want to hurry up my expiration, though I have thought that way at times. I'm just saying I won't be giving up all that much when it finally comes to pass. And I don't imagine anybody'll be mourning my earthly remains neither, which suits me perfect. Just throw whatever's left in the dump and cover it up with more dirt.

CHAPTER 47

Sam

WITH THE COMBINATION OF the soreness that remains from the injuries I sustained in that assault and the pain administered by the inimical seats on this reeking bus, there is not an inch of my body that isn't in profound agony. It feels as though my blood has been drained and replaced by pure liquid pain. My feet have been frozen solid for the entire day, my stomach is clenching, and my face and neck feel as though someone's pounding them with a burning log. If only I could transfer some of the heat from my face to my frostbitten toes.

Even to a young and healthy body these seats would seem like meticulously designed devices of torture. The first thing you notice is that you simply cannot lean back, and that your head, in particular, is forced into an unnatural forward position so that, unless you force your head back the entire time, your chin is pressing against your chest. Before long you realize your legs are confined in far too small a space, and that stretching them out, even for a second, is completely out of the question, which, for reasons I can't comprehend, makes you want to stretch them out all the more. When you attempt to sit up straight, you find your entire torso toppling forward, but when you slink down and bend your lower back, your knees are forced against the unforgiving back of the seat in front of you, where another poor soul is undoubtedly squirming and complaining, if only inwardly. No matter how you stretch, when the bus finally stops and you have a moment to get off and walk around, it takes less than five brief, uncomfortable minutes back in your seat for your lower back to begin to cry out with agony once again. And with every restless minute the ache increases. You might, in desperation, attempt to lean to one side or another, but if you make that particular error you'll quickly learn that the armrests, which only a steel-skinned mutant could properly employ for their putative function, exist for one reason alone: to gouge your ribs with their inflexible metal edges and force you back into the position in which you began this terrible eternal dance.

Surely, that should be enough to satisfy any self-respecting sadist, but of course the horror doesn't end there. For some reason I cannot fathom, no matter how warm the bus is, and it is often stiflingly hot, your feet, which have nowhere to go, are numb with the cold that seems to pour up through the humming floor. Add to all of that the toxic fumes that somehow find their way into the bus and then into your beleaguered lungs and soon enough into your stomach, and you've got a uniquely gruesome form of transportation. After what can't have been more than an hour onboard I was eager to confess to whatever crime I'd been falsely accused of so that they could release me from this evil contraption and put me swiftly to death. Enough.

I don't know what time it is—maybe three o'clock in the morning, maybe later—but the snow is so thick and constant now that the other vehicles, what few there are on the highway at this godforsaken hour, crawl by like mechanical bugs in the snow-peppered blackness, their muted lights shivering as if from the cold as they gradually approach. And then, if you turn your head and follow as they pass, the dim red lights that replace them fade and finally dissolve into the raging whiteness of the storm. And the wind has grown since we left Pittsburgh, spraying the windows with an increasingly dense, icy mix, then whisking it greedily away seconds later. In the most powerful gusts even this massive bus is buffeted about like an overinflated balloon.

At least I've learned a little more about Chick these last couple days, a little more about how he came to this desolate life. He won't share the details with me, and he's never placed blame on anyone but himself, but I now know that something happened years ago, some tragedy that stole from him whatever chance he might have had to lead a normal life. He is plagued by some ancient remorse, scarred, I think, from a life of self-hatred. Maybe, given his humble beginnings, it would have been difficult enough for him anyway, but it seems that some dark episode ended long ago any hopes he might have had for peace or happiness.

I can't help but wonder what would have become of him if not for the burden he's borne. Certainly he is uneducated, and to say he's insufficiently sophisticated would be akin to saying an earthworm is insufficiently winged, but he is neither stupid nor cruel and I've come to value his qualities far more highly than sophistication. In fact he is gentle at times, and industrious, and he is generous with the little he can lay his hands on. It seems a terrible waste of a kind and decent human being. But what gives me, or anyone, the right to say a life such as his has been wasted? And if there is still time for me to find some purpose, who's to say there isn't time for him?

CHAPTER 48

Chick

I GUESS I MUST OF BEEN unconscious for a time, cause I don't rightly recall the crash proper, or how I ended up laying smack dab on top of the young fella who was sitting across the aisle from me before it happened. It was still kind of warm in the bus when I woke up and the lights inside was still glowing, so it couldn't of been for more than few minutes. First voice I heard was Sam's, and he was kind of taking control of the situation, checking people's injuries, telling them all to stay calm and whatnot. To my mind, he seemed like a whole nother person, talking almost normal and making good sense and all. Now, we both of us probably know more about how to stay warm in cold weather than all them other passengers put together, and I got a feeling they figured that out pretty quick, cause they was all of a sudden treating us with a much friendlier attitude. You might even say we was getting a bit of respect from some of them. Old Sam there was real impressive, and no two ways about it. He was tying homemade turner kits on folks who was bleeding and making splinters out of luggage for broken bones and just generally acting like somebody who's right at home leading a platoon of injured soldiers or watching out for a campground of scared kids.

Now, I'm happy to report that most of us wasn't hurt too awful bad, but there was this one little girl who was bleeding *real* profuse. Problem was, her dad wasn't about to let Sam get close enough to take care of her. Well, I couldn't hardly believe what I was seeing, but old Sam puts his face right up close to this guy's face and he says, real firm and serious-like, "I will not stand by and watch another child die." Then he squints his eyes and gets a kind of confused look on his face. I can see his lips trembling like some folks' hands tend to do when they're nervous or after a night of serious drinking. "A*noth*er child?" the girl's father says. Then Sam blinks his eyes and puts his hand on the guy's shoulder and says, "Please. *Please* let me help your little girl."

CHAPTER 49

Claire

THERE ARE LITERALLY hundreds of books offering support and advice to people struggling to cope with everything from minor transient crises to fatal illnesses to the debilitating effects of the most horrendous types of tragedies, but there isn't a single book explaining how to deal with the pain of learning that your only remaining parent no longer recognizes you. Believe me, I've searched the shelves and the Internet dozens, maybe hundreds of times. I suppose I should be relieved to know there's not much of a market. And what would they say? "Feel the pain"? "Embrace the anger"? I don't suppose there's any good way to deal with any of what's happened to us. But of course that's the problem: there is no more us.

I knew before the doctors did, before he'd even recovered his voice. What he couldn't say with his mouth his eyes clearly declared: "I don't know who you are, little girl. I can't help you. It's kind of you to come and visit me, to talk with me and sit by my bed, but I can't give you whatever it is that you need."

What I don't know, what I'll never know, is exactly when that door in his mind fell shut. Was it that night, or was it when he regained consciousness and was reminded that his wife and son were dead? Would everything be different if my face had been the first one he'd seen when he wakened in the hospital or did his memories of a loving family seep out of the slit in his neck along with so much of his blood? I guess it doesn't matter much now, but I might feel just a little better, no, a little less awful, if I were certain that nothing we could have done would have made any difference, because in addition to the sadness and the anger, there has always been guilt; not devastating, debilitating guilt, but a constant subdued gnawing at the already ragged edges of my heart.

Of course my therapist would say that this is all completely normal; in fact she *did* say it, repeatedly. And maybe it is, but I don't think it serves the same purpose for me that it might have at first. I think it's just become another way to keep him in my heart, like fitting him into a dream where he really has no role to play. Sad, precious dreams.

Let it go, Claire. Your kids need you. Thank God for my joyful kids.

CHAPTER 50

Chick

IT WASN'T EASY, BUT WE made it through the night, huddled together like a damn bunch of crippled castaways in that wrecked-up old Greyhound stuck in a snowdrift the size of a schoolhouse a couple hundred yards off the highway. Some of the passengers was in kind of bad shape, what with broken bones and then frostbite and all, but from what the doctors has been saying it looks like we're all going to make it. Oh yeah, and the little girl? They say she lost a lot of blood, which we already knew, but she'll be okay.

Now I ain't seen Sam yet, but they tell me they got him all fixed up pretty good too. Course then, they been asking me a lot of questions about him, like, do I know his name and what happened to his neck and all. Seems like maybe them kids did him more harm than either of us figured, cause they asked me more than once about this big scar. Anyways, I can't wait to see what he looks like without that face full of shag carpeting. I guess they're being extra careful, but they say we both of us'll be up and around in a day or two. Then I imagine we'll have to get back on the road.

Them Greyhound bigwigs has been here too, trying to make sure we don't sue them right out of business I guess. What am I going to do, blame them on the snowstorm? Or verca vica? Looks like if nobody sues them they're going to pay all our hospital bills, get us where we're going, and give us each a few bucks to boot, though I figure they're a bit more interested in getting our signatures on them there promissory notes than paying us off. Still in all, I don't suppose I'll be turning down any offers they'd care to make. I ain't a complete and total idiot.

CHAPTER 51

Sam

THIEVES. GODLESS THIEVES and criminals. Who do they think they are, to take a wizard's beard and toss it in the trash like so much refuse? A wizard without a beard. Pish!

They've tried to force me to look at my reflection, but I am adamant in my refusal. And it's not that I'm afraid. It's the indignity. And now there's all this patter among the doctors and nurses about my neck.

"How did you get that scar?" they ask me.

"A gang of youngsters attacked us with a bat in the last city where we stopped," I respond.

"No, not the bruise on your jaw; the great long scar across your neck."

"Scar?" I answer, with, I hope, appropriate derision.

"A bolt of lightning, perhaps," I say. "Or the mark of a lesser wizard's assault, a lucky blow." What do I care for that? Scar or no scar, beard or no beard, there is important work to do, and I am prepared to do whatever I must to forestall the stranger's doom.

CHAPTER 52

Chick

JESUS CHRIST!

Jesus Christ Almighty.

I got a real sick feeling in my guts as soon as I seen that ugly scar he had hid under all of that goddamn hair. Course I had to study his craggy old face for a couple long minutes before I finally started to dig out the face I seen that night. It's been a awful long time, but there it was, there it was under all the sags and crags and creases going this way and that like what you'd maybe see in old porcelain figures. I come as close to fainting as a man can get and still keep his feet right there underneath him and I nearly shit myself too. It's him and no two ways about it. And yet there ain't no way in hell it *can* be him unless he come back from the dead. I seen that poor son of a bitch with my own eyes. He was lying dead on the floor next to his dead wife, his neck pouring blood out like a old crankcase leaking oil. I can't for the life of me figure how he could of survived with that big old gash in his neck, but then I guess some people's just pure unlucky. Whole goddamn situation gives me a case of the shivers and makes me all sick inside too. Jesus Christ. Jesus Christ almighty on a beanstock. I'm right back in hell and I paid for the ticket to get me here. Jesus.

I know I must of turned some kind of pale green color when I finally realized who I was gawking at, cause he right away asked me what they done to me to get me looking so awful, like he was going to go after them doctors for hurting me. That made me feel even worse. Least I know now he ain't no wizard, and he ain't reading my mind and there ain't no hypnotist detective neither, whatever good that does me. Sad fact of it is the poor son of a bitch is reading his own damned mind, and he ain't got a clue in the whole world who I am or what he's been through. Not yet anyways.

I ain't no cycle analyst, but the way I got it figured he don't remember none of what happened that night, least not right up in the front of his brain. But somewheres, way in the back there, high up on a shelf where there ain't been no light nor air for a long time, he's got the whole thing stored up, and I'll allow some of it's starting to seep through for one reason or the other. Who the hell knows, maybe it's my fault for bumping into him. Seems like I can't stop doing damage no matter what the hell I do.

Now, could I be mistaken? Well, every time I start thinking I might be making this up or having a hallucination cause of how guilty I feel, I just take another look at him and there it is right in front of me, the living, breathing truth. My heart's still pounding like a bass drum in a fast-motion parade.

Now what in the damned hell am I supposed to do?

CHAPTER 53

Claire

OF COURSE IT ISN'T JUST the loss of my father that plagues me; I think about my mother and my little brother every day of my life. The difference is that I know they are dead—I saw their bodies, I mourned the losses and mourned them again. They couldn't be here with me if they wanted to and there is not a thing in the world I can do for them.

With my father it's different. He may still be out there somewhere, he may need me, and God knows I've needed him. As terrible as it might sound, his death would probably have been easier for me to take, in some ways, than was his disappearance. Though I sometimes feel I can find some way to put it all behind me and move on, I just can't seem to let go of the idea that he might be alive, however unlikely I know that is.

I know he wasn't well when he left, but he was relatively young and could have recovered. Could he be married again, living with a new name, a new wife, a new brood of children that he loves as much as he once loved us? It seems terribly improbable, but there is no way to know, no way I can be absolutely certain. He could be lying in some awful prison cell, or rotting in an asylum somewhere. Is there something I could do if I knew how to find him? Something I could do to comfort him? Some way to ease his pain? Maybe just hold his hand. Even if he still didn't recognize me, wouldn't it be good for him to know that someone cares?

It's not so difficult to be alone, to isolate yourself, if you're living a relatively normal life. How much harsher the world must be if you don't know who you are, where you're from, or that someone somewhere loves you, that someone truly needs you. A life without context, like a bird in flight with no place to land.

CHAPTER 54

Chick

IT'S A EERIE, KIND OF sickening feeling when you find out you know more about somebody than they know about their own selves. Specially when what you know is as terrible as what I know about old Sam. As much as you'd might want to help them figure out who they are, you know for sure there ain't nothing you could say would cause them more hurt than the simple, honest truth. What worries me now is he seems hell-bent on finding out for his own self, and I somehow got myself all mixed up in trying to help him. Now *there's* a sad situation. Well, if he's real lucky I'll be as bad at that as I been at just about everything else I put my rotten mind to.

CHAPTER 55

Claire

HERE IS SOME OF WHAT I remember about my father. I remember a tall, broad-shouldered man, although it may just be because I was a little girl then, that from where I stood he seemed so immense, so powerful. Of course I remember his face, his brown hair and eyes, his mischievous smile and disheveled hair, but even if I didn't have a mental picture there would still be the photographs. His voice, which was altered by the injury he received in the attack, was seldom raised, though Timmy and I knew very well when he was serious. We knew when it was time to behave, and we knew just as well that as soon as we settled down he would forgive whatever minor infraction we'd committed and life would go back to normal.

Dad loved to share his knowledge; you could see it in his smile, in the glimmer in his eyes. With a degree in English and his years of studying astrophysics he could easily have been a college professor, but instead he chose to work as a grade school principal. And he was a born actor, always playing parts to entertain us. There was a part of him that was very childlike. Every Fourth of July he would put on a fireworks demonstration for all the children in the neighborhood and any students who wanted to attend. He was enthralled by nature, by the sky, by almost everything, or so it seemed to me. We spent so many evenings in the backyard, looking at the stars or catching lightning bugs in our mason jars, tiny holes poked in the lids so they wouldn't suffocate before we released them. Wherever we were, whatever we were doing, it seemed as though my father always had one hand resting lightly on my head.

Certainly my parents' relationship wasn't perfect, but I never had any real concerns about our family's future. I never feared that one of them might leave. Parental disputes were resolved quietly, behind closed doors, and in the end they always stood together, at least in front of us.

I can still remember watching my father shave in the morning; I'd run to the bathroom door as soon as I heard the hum of his electric razor and stand there in awe, waiting for him to notice me. If he was in a good mood, which he usually was, and not in too much of a hurry, which was less common, he'd aim the buzzing razor at me and start to lunge in my direction. That was my cue to scurry down the hall, feigning fear while giggling with joy. And seconds later I'd be standing outside the door again, waiting for the next attack.

I remember dinnertime, when my father would talk about his day; he'd always have a humorous story about one or another of the students or teachers at the school, and we would all sit quietly listening until he was finished before sharing our own stories. I don't know if it was because of financial limitations or the limitations of my mother's culinary skills, but there was little variety in our diet from one week to the next. Still, Dad, who Mom always said ate more than most men twice his size, would rarely fail to compliment her on the simple dinners she cooked.

My father's scent, that's what I remember most vividly, and yet that's the most difficult recollection for me to put into words. I imagine it sounds strange, but to me he smelled of nature; perhaps a hint of wood smoke, a touch of spice, a trace of sweet vegetation, not unlike the smell of the deep woods after a summer storm. That's not it, of course, but I believe I'd recognize it if I came across it again. There may be other men who share his scent, but then I seldom come close enough to any man to find out. Or it may be that human scents are like fingerprints, no two identical. That's what I prefer to believe.

CHAPTER 56

Sam

IT'S ALL SUCH A MUDDLE. Unfamiliar faces, flashing knives, gunshots, and blood. I can almost feel the terror in the man's heart. Visions of a tragedy yet to come or has it already passed? How did I get drawn in to this?

It was my final day in that dreadful hospital, and I was alone in my room, dressed in my own clothes again and eager to move on when I finally yielded and faced the mirror. I suppose I look cleaner than I did with the beard, more respectable, but there is something unsettling about the image that frowns back at me whenever I dare to steal another furtive glance. I look less like a wizard, and more like a man—an old man, buckling under the weight of time.

And it seems I'm not the only one who's changed. Chick has grown a little distant since the accident. He swears there is nothing wrong, but I can see that he's troubled. Today, as we boarded the bus for the final leg of our journey, he took my arm and turned me toward him. "Maybe I was wrong," he said, his eyes nervously avoiding mine. "Wrong about what, Chick?" I asked. "Maybe I was just imagining that guy you're looking to save. Maybe we should go on back to good old Muncie where we know our way around."

I tried to explain that he was just the conduit through which the information was being delivered to me, but he seemed unwilling to listen. He reminded me of our little room under the steps, as if I might have forgotten. "We might never find us so good a home as what we had," he said, and I believe I detected a note of genuine sorrow in his tone.

I suppose it makes sense that he would have reservations. With all that's happened to us since we left Muncie, even I have had occasion to question the wisdom of moving on, but in spite of all of that, and in spite of the sense of foreboding that's been stalking me, I no longer feel I have any choice but to play it out, to see where it takes me. Yes, I am torn, conflicted between the nameless fears of what might lie ahead for me and the irresistible gravitational pull of this stranger's plight. But I cannot, I will not allow myself the option of a retreat. With all I've lost to the passing of time I simply can't abide the thought of surrendering whatever is left of my dignity or allowing suffering I might have the capacity to forestall. And I have developed a deep feeling for the man for whom we are searching. It's as though he were a long-lost brother, a twin I didn't know I had. Whatever the forces and feelings that have brought me here, I must follow my heart. Indeed I have little else.

CHAPTER 57

Chick

FOR ABOUT A MINUTE THERE it was like Sam and me was celebrities, heroes I guess you'd say. Most all the folks who was on the bus with us when it crashed come by to say their thank-yous and fare-thee-wells before we left the hospital. Some of them's still laid up, and a couple just went on their way, I guess, but there's more than one or two right here on the bus with us, and you can tell just by how they look at us they're holding us in what you could call a higher esteem than what they had before the crash. Fact is, when you think about it, there wasn't nothing too special about what we done, taking care of them people and helping them keep warm and all. I guess it's just that they wasn't figuring us for the sort of folks would be most likely to take charge of that kind of situation, or maybe any other, for that matter. Course then who's better equipped to get through what you'd call less than perfect circumstances than a couple old fellows been surviving on the streets most of their lifes? Anyways, it was old Sam who really took charge and did most of the work. He was the real star of the show, so to say, and the truth is I'm glad of it. I ain't used to the spotlight and don't much care for the kind of heat it throws.

At first them doctors and such at the hospital was winding up to give us a hard time cause Sam and me wouldn't give them

137

no last names, but I think they finally just give up out of flustration. Then, when we had to sign the papers for the bus company, we had to go through the whole damn rigmarole again. I think they was afraid we was trying to pull something sneaky on them so's we could say we didn't sign nothing and maybe sue them for the accident at a later date. Seems these lawyer types gets more than a little confused when something don't quite fit in with what they come to expect. It was actually kind of funny watching them get all heated up and squirming and turning colors and such. In the end we just made up some names and swore to them, which we should of did right up front.

What I come to realize while all of this was going on was I'm the only one knows Sam's real name, his first name anyways. Still remember his wife calling out for Stephen just before Phil slit her throat. And I ain't told nobody my own real name for I don't know how long. It just don't seem wise nor prudent neither, and truth is I don't really feel like that person's alive no more. He was pretty much lost that same night.

Anyways, much as it worries me, we're going to be pulling into Scranton in about a hour. Then, I don't know what the hell's going to happen. Probably nothing. Probably Sam's so far gone now he'll never have to remember what he seen. Truth to be told, that's what I'm hoping, because if he *is* heading for something more than that, I can't see how whatever he's heading for could do him much good. I sure as shit ain't chomping at the bit to see that old neighborhood, but I don't know what the hell else I'm supposed to do. I mean, I ain't too good even in what you might call usual circumstances, and these circumstances is about as usual as a pair of eyeballs peering out of a hairy asshole.

Who knows what he'll do if I go ahead and take him back to his old house? If he starts remembering who he is and what happened, he might need hisself some kind of wizard just to keep him from ending up in the loony bin, that is if he don't off hisself first like some folks does when they can't take what they been dealt, like I maybe should have done years ago. The way I got it figured, there's some things we just ain't designed to cope with. And anyways, what's the point of his finding out now, when there ain't a thing in the wide world for him to do but howl and holler till he can't howl and holler no more? That don't get you nothing but a sore throat and a lot of funny looks. I know that from my own experience. The more I think about this, the dumber it seems. Maybe it ain't too late to change my mind, just tell him I screwed up, or disappear in the night. I done that before. I just wasn't made for this.

CHAPTER 58

Sam

CHICK HAS LEFT ME ALONE here on a bench in the courthouse square. I am to wait for him while he searches for the man we've come to rescue. Strangely, he seems to have taken charge now, but what is perhaps even stranger is that I've allowed him to do so. There may be no clearer sign of my increasing senility than that I've put myself into the hands of this uneducated man about whom I know almost nothing in hopes of finding a man about whom I know even less. And yet he is convinced that between my talking in my sleep, his knowledge of the area, and what he describes, perhaps quite accurately, as his own psychotic rumblings, he has some knowledge to which I am not privy, some knowledge that will make it possible to continue in my quest, and so I sit here, cold and weary, but cleaner and, in spite of my scars and bruises, more respectable in appearance than I've been for many years. When he returns, he told me as he headed out to who knows where, he plans to find us inexpensive lodging, which we can pay for with the small sum of money we accepted from the team of smarmy barristers who represented the bus company.

Something else. He has insisted that I continue to shave. In fact he threatened to shave me in my sleep if I refused to comply with his unexplained and, in my opinion, completely unreasonable command. Why this particular issue has taken on such importance for him I cannot even begin to imagine, but he has been good to me, so I have reluctantly consented, at least for now. After all, the damage has already been done.

From the little I've seen so far, Scranton is remarkably unremarkable, a dingy gray wound of a city surrounded by rolling brown hills whose wooded shoulders are cloaked in what seems a constant cover of low winter clouds. There might be some respite from the harshness of urban life hidden deep in those distant hills, but if you keep your gaze low you could be in almost any city in the country. What did I expect? I suppose I expected to be overcome by a palpable sense that there was something important here. I thought perhaps I would feel in my very core that we had reached our intended destination. Instead, what I feel is a hint of depression and some distant indescribable force gently tugging at the bruised core of my heart. I am more confused now than ever. Oh yes, and my back is acting up again. I can move about, but not without extra effort and considerable pain.

And so I wait, while my enigmatic partner does whatever it is he's doing. I am so very tired.

CHAPTER 59

Chick

I CAN'T HELP BUT NOTICE IT. This town just don't appear much like what I remember it to of been. They set down buildings and roads where they didn't have none before, and on the edges of the city, where there used to be just fields and forest, they put up big old highways and such. Funny thing is, for all the constructing they done, the city don't look one whole hell of a lot more attractive than it used to. And to my mind that ain't saying much in the way of a compliment. I guess it's just sort of a fancier, moderner version of what it always was. Course it might look better from a higher position, like probably most things does when you get far enough away.

Now I thought I had me a pretty fair recollection of where I used to live, and I figured once I got there I could find my way to Sam's old house, but I didn't realize getting to my old neighborhood was going to get so damn complicated, or being there was going to make me feel so damn itchy and peculiar. When I finally got there, I must of stood staring up at my rickety old house for a good hour or more. Fact of it is, people started peeking out their windows and doors at me, like I was casing the neighborhood or such as that. Course then I was just about the only white fella in the general vicinity, far as I could tell. But there was one young fella, probably eleven or twelve years old from the look of him, eyeing me from a upstairs window, looking blank and empty, like he was already out of hope. I just wanted to tell him not to give up so easy, to yell out to him he could make it if he didn't go wrong, if he just wrestled his way out from under whatever was weighing him down. Then I thought how stupid that'd sound coming from an old bum like me. I don't come to tears easy, but I could of cried right then.

What I come to learn is you never know how you're going to feel till your right smack dab in the middle of a particular situation. My memory's been so filled up with that one event I couldn't quite see around it, so to say, but I figured when I come face-to-face with the house I was born and raised in it'd maybe jiggle my memory some about other stuff, maybe some happy memories and such. Well sir, no such luck. Sure, I got a funny feeling in my guts, like a big old ball of worms rolling around, but I still couldn't remember nothing specific. Course then, maybe it's just as well. What's past is probably better left past, least for the most part.

Anyways, with all the different bus routes running up one side of the city and down the other, I can't make heads nor tails of how to get out to Sam's old house. On the other hand I ain't sure how hard I been trying. If I really put my mind to it, I could maybe find the place before dark, but damn it, I just ain't quite ready yet. I just ain't. It's getting late and I'm tired and who knows what kind of trouble old Sam's got hisself into downtown where he don't know east from west or north from down.

I don't know. Maybe I can still find some reasonable way to slither out of this damn thing. I mean, what the hell am I trying to prove anyways? Sure, I could go look at that house and see if I feel any better, or any worse, which is more likely and maybe what I'm hoping for, but I don't need to put that old man through any more than he's already been through. If I want to torture myself, that's fine I guess, but I done enough to him already.

CHAPTER 60

Claire

WHEN THIS BLEAK WINTER weather moves in, I find myself wanting to curl up into a ball and cover my head with blankets until spring. Life is cold and drab enough without the tactile and visual reminders. I know I can't stay home, and yet going to work and facing my students and colleagues requires such enormous effort. But I refuse to go into hibernation again. I will not allow myself the inviting, suffocating comfort of self-destruction. Survival is the only vengeance, perhaps the only victory I'll ever know, and it's the only way I have to keep my brother's laughter echoing, my parents' fading seed alive.

CHAPTER 61

Chick

I'M SHOOK. I'M SHOOK SO BAD I'm afraid my heart's going to up and explode. I figured when I realized who Sam was that that'd be the biggest shock I'd ever go through, except for that night, of course. Turns out I was wrong again, and wrong *big*-time. This one's got me so knotted up inside I can't hardly think a clear thought. I ain't took a easy breath since it happened and I maybe never will. I don't even know how to start. I know what I seen, but it just don't make no kind of sense. It's like I'm having some kind of hallucinations, but everything else seems pretty much normal in my brain far as I can tell, least as normal as it's ever been.

Probably shouldn't have did it, but I got us a cheap hotel room downtown last night so's we could stay warm and rest up a little more before we do whatever it is we think we're doing. Once you get yourself a taste of the creaturely comforts, you don't much feel like going back to sleeping on the sidewalk. We was both pretty quiet, and maybe a little moody, mostly trying to just stay out of each other's way, I guess. I got up early, cause even with the real beds and the heat and all I was all restless and fidgety. I thought Sam was still sleeping when I was getting ready to head out, but then he all of a sudden sits up and says to me, "Are we

145

going today to rescue the man who's summoned me?" or some such thing. I told him I needed a little more time to find this guy. He didn't much like having to wait, and he actually got a little testy for a minute, but I was able to slip out before he could cause too big of a ruckus.

Well, after finding my own neighborhood yesterday, it wasn't too much trouble, once I finally set my mind to it, figuring out the bus routes to what used to be Sam's house. But there ain't no way I was prepared for what I seen. After I got my bearings and found the right block, I wandered around studying them houses from different angles just to be sure as I could be I was at the right place. I found the house and I was just sort of loitering around trying not to look too suspicious and trying not to think too much about what went on in there when this van pulls up in front of the house and stops. About a second later this big guy gets out and goes up this sort of ramp thing to the front porch and rings the doorbell. After another minute or two, the door opens and this woman comes rolling out in a wheelchair. Well, I don't pay her too much mind till she gets close enough so's I can see her face features nice and clear. And who do you think she looks like? I'll be damned if she don't look like a modern version of the poor woman what used to live there, the one got her throat sliced that night, Sam's, or rather Stephen's wife. Now her hair's done up different, and she ain't quite so thin as what I remember, plus which, she should of been older by a goodly amount if it was her, but still in all, there's a powerful resemblance and no two ways about it. Course I know good and well it can't be her, cause there wasn't no question in nobody's mind that lady was dead, all sprawled out there on the floor and spilling out blood. I might of been wrong about Sam, but that lady wasn't getting up, and I'd bet my teeth, each and every rotten one, on it.

Well, after the guy rolls her chair up into the van and leaves and I finally catch my breath and force my heart back down my gullet, I start to figure I maybe know who she is after all. I suppose it could be there was a little baby girl in the house we none of us seen that night, but more likely this'd be that same little girl was hiding up on them steps, the one Phil was going to make Lenny kill when I up and run off. I figured Lenny'd have to do what Phil said, cause he was as scary as I ever seen him, but then I never seen with my own eyes what happened. Now, I don't know did them guys do something to cripple her up like that or did that come later, or maybe is this just a temporary condition from a car accident or the like. I can't for the life of me figure why she'd still be living here, but sure as shit stinks when it's fresh and steamy, that's gotta be that same poor little girl I seen sitting at the top of the stairs watching her family get slaughtered, one by one.

CHAPTER 62

Claire

FOR JUST A MOMENT THIS morning I felt a hint of hope, but it fled as swiftly as it came, another sparrow on the windowsill. When I came outside, a man was loitering in front of the house, just standing by the old oak at the edge of the yard. He was an odd-looking man, disheveled, nervous, and a little suspicious, and of course I immediately thought of father. But it wasn't him. It never is.

There's always something—something that would be obvious if I weren't so desperate, or if it hadn't been so long. The hair is too dark, the shoulders too narrow, the nose too small, the walk not quite right. There's always something. Of course I don't really know what he would look like today; I can't be sure I would even recognize him if I saw him on the street. I only know when it isn't him.

My students are waiting. My life is rushing by.

CHAPTER 63

Chick

IT TOOK ME A GOOD LONG while to absorb what I seen and what it might of meant, but once I got my brain wrapped good and tight around the idea that she's who I figure she is, I realized I got no choice now, no choice at all. I mean, even if he is disordered in his mind, and maybe she's crippled up, so to say, it seems to me I gotta try and put the two of them together one way or the other. I know better than anyone how I tend to fuck things up once I set my mind to it, but I can't see no way around this one. Maybe I can someway do something for them people I hurt so bad, leastwise the ones who's still alive and breathing. I know I might someday regret this too, but I just don't see how I got a choice now and I guess you could say regret's my normal condition.

Now on the other hand, I could end up getting myself in some kind of serious trouble, and even if I don't, there's a better than even chance they's both going to end up hating me if and when they come to find out who I am. They got every right and reason, but I'm still going to feel pretty bad losing old Sam as a friend and companion. It ain't just that I feel terrible for what I done to him, or I feel sorry cause of what he's been through. I come to feel a real close sort of fond affection for him. Underneath all of his crazy talk and odd kind of behavior, I'd say he's got

149

hisself some real fine qualities. I wish now I'd knowed him before what happened happened. Maybe I could of even found some way to stop it then. Maybe I might of been a different kind of person my *own* self. Course what I mean to say is a better person. Probably that ain't so likely as I'd wish to believe.

CHAPTER 64

Sam

SOMETHING IS TERRIBLY AMISS. The images speed by now, like automobiles on a highway spinning out of control, and they assault me during the day and throughout the night. People are dead; people are dying. The man is screaming out, the boy's face is . . . is exploding. Everything is terribly wrong.

Last night was the worst by far. The silk scarf became a river of blood, the child's face disintegrated a dozen times, and the man let out a growl such as I've never heard before. In all my years of living on the street I haven't felt such chilling cold; in all my years of running from thugs and hoodlums, from nightmares and real dangers, I've never felt such pure stark terror. In my dreams I was the man, or he was me, or perhaps we were each other. I was helpless inside him, desperate but unable to bring an end to our recurring nightmare, struggling to escape. And for just a second I saw his eyes, so much like my own, yet younger and charged with dread. Too much like my own.

I'm almost ashamed to admit it, even to myself, but when I wakened this morning I felt such a powerful need for succor that I desired nothing more than the tender touch of a caring hand, any hand. I wanted to beg Chick to come and sit by me, to put his hand on my head and tell me it's okay, to hold me like a baby if he could stomach the thought. Of course I couldn't utter the words, couldn't ask him to comfort me. How does one ask for such a simple thing? How can a man confess to such a simple basic need without appearing weak?

Is it simple pride that stifles me? Is it the need to be, or to at least feel as though I am in control, to deny the humanity I inherited after the fall? Is it so shameful to feel pain, so disgraceful to confess frailty or need? Whatever I was, I'm nothing more than a lost man now, weary and afraid, afraid for myself and for the stranger who visits my dreams, uninvited. Could he just be a figment, a specter brought on by malnutrition, old age, and alcohol abuse? Could I be deluding myself? One minute I am certain of my mission; the next it seems nothing more than a childish fancy. I want to stop now, but even if I'm only a man, how can I take the risk? If the slightest possibility exists that I can come to the aid of some tortured soul, how can I retreat? I couldn't live with myself if I thought I'd allowed that suffering to go on when I might have stopped or even eased it. Whatever life remains for me, I'd like to live it without self-recrimination, without the fear that when the end finally comes I'll suddenly recognize my insignificance, the utter comic futility of my existence. What if I am not what I believe I am? What if I never was? What if that is all I have left to learn?

So again I wait on the streets of this dull gray city, my back throbbing, while Chick goes about his mysterious business. I wait and hope we are here for a reason, that it is not too late and that I can do something to stave off the tragedy that shreds my sleep. And though the dreams are a torment to me, I fear now that they may be only a pale shadow of the brutal reality they depict. I am only an observer of a horror that barely glances me. It is the other man, the stranger, who truly stands to suffer. If only I could touch him, give him the comfort I awoke desiring. But now I doubt everything. Everything seems a dream. Are we all this helpless and alone? If we are, do we really need to be reminded?

CHAPTER 65

Chick

I COULD COME UP EASY with a couple hundred damn good reasons not to go through with it. I could just hightail it out of here right now and go on with my stupid goddamn life the same way I done up to now. It ain't much, but I could leave Sam what's left of the money and quick disappear and nobody'd ever be the wiser. Sam would most likely go on just like he's done up to now, and that pretty lady in the wheelchair would go on doing whatever it is she does, and that'd be the end of it. Nothing I can do is going to make me forget what I done, and nothing's going to change what I am, or what Sam is or what she is neither.

Still in all, it don't seem to matter how much I argue with myself, I can't see how I got much choice now. I told myself I was going to face the damage I done, and when I realized who Sam was I promised myself I'd take care of him, least as good as I could. Maybe I don't know what's best, but it seems to me they both of them got a right to know the other one's alive. And ain't no one else around to inform them but me. And then too, they might require someone to stick their hate and anger onto. Who knows, maybe if they hate me enough, I won't need to hate my own self so much. Or maybe that's just hopeful thinking, but it really don't matter cause my feelings don't enter into it, or least-wise they shouldn't. I guess I'm going to do what I'm going to do and be done with it once and for all. Now I just want an end, an end to everything.

PART THREE

CHAPTER 66

Sam, Chick, Claire

ON AN AGE-WORN PARK bench near the edge of the faded lawn that surrounds the Scranton courthouse, Sam sits alone, his arms folded snugly against his chest, his eyes combing the snow-speckled ground, scattered remains of the flurries that fell off and on throughout the night.

"Sam," Chick calls out from the sidewalk. Slowly, he approaches his shivering companion.

Sam glances up. His face is pale, and his pink-rimmed eyes are cloaked in a thin glaze of tears spawned by the icy wind. "I'm growing more impatient with each passing minute, my friend," he says. "And I fear time is running short, if it isn't already too late."

"Okay," Chick says, and he shifts from one foot to the other like a nervous child. "Well, I'm pretty sure I found the house, so I figure we can just go on ahead out there and then just wait there till somebody or the nother shows up." He says this to the ground.

Sam nods and, grasping the bench with both hands, lifts himself to his feet.

Side by side, the two men walk to the corner, where, after a few minutes have passed, a grimy blue and white bus rumbles to a stop, its door jerking open like a mechanical jaw. Fifteen minutes later they board a second bus, and following a wordless five-minute ride and a brief wait, they board a third, which climbs a long steep hill before continuing onto a rolling two-lane road lined with strip malls, gas stations, bars, and a seemingly random assortment of trees and shrubbery. Shortly after the forest has swallowed up the last of the city's tendrils, Chick presses the tape and a tone sounds in the front of the bus. A minute later the bus slows and pulls over to the shoulder of the road, where it lurches to a squeaking halt. The rear doors flap open and two men step out into the arctic air. Still silent, they stand watching as the bus pulls away, a dusty wake rising and falling behind it like a sheet in the wind.

With their hands thrust deep in their pockets, the two make their way through a maze of suburban streets, neither man speaking a word. When they reach the house, Chick notices for the first time the name on the mailbox that sits at the end of the cement walkway leading to the porch.

"Ring any kind of bells?" he asks, gesturing toward the mailbox, mostly hoping now that it won't.

"The mailbox? I'm afraid I haven't seen it before. If this is the home, I've seen only the inside, a staircase and a single room, in fact. Is this the man's name?" Sam runs his crooked fingers over the raised letters. The name on the box is Mallory.

"Yeah." Chick sighs and swallows. "I'm guessing it most likely is."

Together they tramp along the path toward the wheelchair ramp and the porch steps that abut it on the right. They climb the three steps to the porch and stand shivering for a moment, neither one quite ready now to make the next move, neither one able to decide what the next move should be. Chick straightens his baggy overcoat before approaching the door. Tentatively, he reaches out, his fingers trembling, and presses the doorbell. They wait, and when there is no response, he rings the bell again.

"I guess it's still kind of early," Chick says. "Or maybe late." And so they remain there while the gray sky gradually dims.

◆ ◆ ◆

As is her ritual, Claire has spent the majority of the ride looking back on her day and falling in and out of a welcome but disorienting half-sleep, the sights and sounds of the commute mingling with unrelated scraps of memory and foreshortened dreams. Only after the van's hydraulic lift has deposited her onto the sidewalk in front of her home and the van has pulled away from the curb does she notice the two shabby figures waiting side by side on her porch, their faces cloaked in shadow. For just a second she feels a tightness in her chest, like the contraction of an overburdened muscle. But then she remembers how swiftly disappointment displaces hope.

Slowly, she makes her way up the cement path to the bottom of the ramp that leads to her front porch. When she sees his craggy face in the light, there is a second of uncertainty, then a moment of disbelief. And then the hope rises inside her.

There are no words now for Claire, and if there were it wouldn't matter. She cannot speak; she cannot move at all. She is hovering untethered, suspended in time, terrified that anything she says or does will dissolve the image she still isn't entirely certain she's seeing. There is only this moment, this impossible, fragile moment.

Chick is the first to speak. "It's okay, Ma'am," he says. "We ain't going to hurt you none."

She is falling again, falling through the darkness. And then something snaps and Claire's tears begin to flow.

"Oh my God," Sam cries, and covers his face with his hands. "We're too late," he says. "It's already happened."

Still Claire says nothing. Weeping now like a terrified child, she struggles to steer her wheelchair toward her father. When her hands refuse to cooperate, Chick comes down to her and positions himself behind the chair. As he wheels her up the ramp, he bends down toward her and says, "I don't believe he knows who you are, Miss, or who he is neither for that matter." She turns her head and squints up at him, the glistening tears streaming down her cheeks, and he can see the confusion on her face. He leans in a little closer and whispers, "When you catch your voice again, you might just want to tell him everything's okay, and not to worry cause he ain't too late."

After another minute passes, and she has partially composed herself, she does what he suggested.

"But then where is the man?" Sam asks when Claire seems calmer. "And if it isn't too late, why are you so distraught?"

"What man?" Claire looks to the stranger for an answer.

"He's been having visions, Ma'am, about some kind of tragedy happening in this here house of yours. He's been seeing the fella who lived . . . the fella who maybe *lives* here and his family get . . . Well he's been seeing some pretty awful stuff. He figures maybe he can someway stop it . . . stop the violence before it happens, so to say." Chick stares at his shoes.

Sam kneels down and addresses the woman face-to-face. "There is a man, possibly your husband, and a child, a handsome little boy with unruly chestnut hair. They're in grave danger, Miss, and you may be too. Certainly there are differences, but this could well be the place, you might be the woman I've come . . . we've come here to protect."

All Claire feels certain of now is that this man is her father and that she isn't willing to risk losing him again. "Please, come inside," she says as evenly as she can. Then she makes her way to the front door.

In the same room where in a single night their lives were shattered, the three sit in taut silence, one recalling images from recent dreams, another flashes from an aborted youth, and the third the gory images that have virtually consumed his soul.

The walls of the living room, once covered with wallpaper, are painted now, pale shades of blue and eggshell. The furniture—a low-backed gray couch, a matching easy chair, a long walnut coffee table, and a series of bookshelves—is modern, functional, and unassuming. Positioned neatly atop a portable entertainment center, flanked by a pair of small rectangular speakers, is a television. And there are books everywhere, though not nearly as many as there once were.

Sam inspects the room for a minute before speaking. "Yes, this could be the house," he says, "though if it is, it has been altered. Or it may be that the changes are yet to come."

"What does it look like?" Claire asks, though she knows the answer. "The house in your dreams," she explains. She glances around her living room, suddenly self-conscious, aware that she's been staring at the distorted remains of her father, a gaunt and ashen shadow of a truant ghost.

"The size and shape of this room appear similar enough to what I've seen, and the door and the staircase each seem to be in their proper location, but the adornments are different, and I don't recall the mechanical contraption that's built into your stairs. Still, I can't deny that sitting here now I feel as though I were engulfed in a mass of human suffering, dense and churning." He takes a deep breath, sighs. "I'm afraid I'm no longer certain what I feel or why?" He leans back.

"I'm sorry," Claire says, looking first at Chick, then back at her father, whose eyes have now fallen shut. "I'm a dreadful hostess. Can I get either of you some coffee, or maybe something to eat? You must be hungry."

Chick clears his throat. "I wouldn't want to put you to no trouble on my account, Ma'am, but I guess I could do with a touch of coffee, that is, if you was already planning to have some your own self."

In her wheelchair, Claire navigates her customary path through the dining room and then through the widened entryway to the kitchen, where she begins to prepare coffee and snacks for her guests.

She is sitting at the small kitchen table, slicing cheese on an old wooden cutting board, when Chick knocks lightly on the doorjamb.

"Could I maybe help you with something?" he asks, trying to appear less uneasy, calmer than he feels.

She motions toward the living room. "Is he okay?"

"Seems he's catching some z's right now, Ma'am. Sleeping I mean to say."

"Well, if you really want to help me with something, maybe

you could tell me how you know my . . . my father, and how you knew to bring him here." She stops slicing for a moment and fixes her gaze on her guest. Her hands, she notices, are shaking. "You did bring him here, didn't you?"

"It's more like I just helped get him where he was already headed."

"Well . . . in any case, I'm indebted to you. I can't tell you how much I appreciate whatever part you played in getting him to me. But there's still so very much I don't know. The fact is I don't know anything at all."

"I'm sorry, Ma'am—"

"Claire," she says, and carves a few more slices of cheese.

"I guess I'd be happy to tell you whatever I know about him, though it probably ain't a whole lot. It's just, I think I'd prefer not to discuss my own personal situation, if you didn't mind too much."

Claire sets the knife down in front of her, pushes the cutting board away from her and regards the stranger she's invited into her home. "I've been without my father for most of my life," she says. "I've wondered every day since he . . . since he disappeared where he was and what he was doing, if he was sober or drunk, if he was still alive or rotting in some ditch." She forces back the tears. "Whatever his condition, his state of mind, he's here now, and I'm more grateful for that than I can possibly put into words."

"Yes, Ma'am."

"I just want to try to help him now, to truly bring him back if I can. I'm not going to quibble with you about what you're willing to divulge about your own life. I guess that's really none of my business anyway. But I'd appreciate it if you'd tell me everything you can about my father."

"Well . . ." He pauses.

"If you want money, I'd be willing to—"

"No, Ma'am," Chick says louder than he intended. "No, Ma'am," he says more calmly. "I don't want none of your money."

"What *do* you want?"

"Well, I guess I mostly want the same as you do, or pretty near, anyways. I'd like to see old Sam get hisself fixed up, and you too for that matter." He runs his eyes over her crippled body and then lets his gaze drift to the kitchen floor. "Leastwise as much as you can."

"Why?" She narrows her eyes. "Why would you want to help either one of us?"

"Well, Ma'am, maybe he is kind of odd sometimes, if you'll pardon my saying it, but he give me a roof over my head and treated me like a brother when he didn't hardly know me from Adam and Eve. And he's always shared anything he had like we was some kind of lifelong cohorts, so to say. You could say I come to care a goodly bit about the crazy . . . I come to care about him."

A smile brightens her face. "It's okay."

"I guess I maybe just want to someway pay him back if I can—"

"I'd really like to hear about it. If you don't mind."

While Sam sits asleep on the couch, Chick tells his story, carefully amended for his audience. He reveals to Claire how he first met her father, how they've been living and how they traveled, and he tells her about the older man's delusions. Describing it as speculation, he hints at what he knows of her father's past, without divulging any hint of the part he played.

"My father's name is Stephen Mallory," Claire says when Chick has finished his story.

Chick grins. "I know it ain't none of my business, but what's his middle name, that is, if you don't mind me asking?"

"Arthur. Why?"

"Well, I'm just sort of guessing of course, but I figure that's most likely where he picked up his wizard moniker."

"I'm sorry?"

"Sam's his initials, Ma'am. All spelled out."

"Yes." Claire smiles. "My father was a grade school principal, a very well-educated man who dearly loved his family. He cherished us," she says, and allows another smile to tug at the corners of her mouth. "Like most fathers, I suppose." She looks up at Chick. "I imagine we were a fairly normal family, but in my mind we'll always be special."

Chick wants to respond, to say something supportive or give some sign that he understands, but he can find no words so he just sits and listens as she continues.

"One night some men broke in, to rob the house, I guess. At some point my mom came down and . . ." She pauses. "She must have surprised them." Unconsciously, she squeezes both hands into fists, then slowly releases them. "I lost both my mother and my little brother that night. The men slit my father's throat and probably assumed he was dead too. And according to the doctors who cared for him afterward, he should have been. I don't really know how long I'd been sitting at the top of the steps when they noticed me. They must have been afraid I could identify them." She shakes her head, snickers, but doesn't smile. "Of course I was in shock. I really didn't have any idea what I'd seen. I still don't remember seeing it. I would have been completely useless as a witness, but then I guess they didn't know that, or didn't care. Who knows what they were thinking. When one of them started up the steps, some part of me . . . whatever part of me was aware must have realized I was in danger. Without thinking about it, I rushed into my room and locked the door behind me.

"Much of what happened that night, much of what I must have seen, is like some awful hazy nightmare—that's all it's ever been—but I can still remember the way the door shook and buckled, and I can remember wrestling with my window and screaming for help before I leapt out into the darkness."

Chick nods and looks away, recalling the scream he'd assumed was her last.

"When I regained consciousness I was in the hospital. Because of the damage the fall had done to my spine, I'd lost the use of my legs. A couple days after learning that, I learned that my father had . . . had lost touch with reality."

"I guess anyone might of did pretty much the same in the situation. Lost their minds I mean."

"Yeah, I suppose that's probably true," she says. "I guess I don't know."

"Well anyways . . ." Chick can't suppress a wince as an image flashes in his mind: a little boy leaps out; a single shot is fired. "Well, it seems to me he's made hisself a past he could sort of block out the real truth with. And I can't say as I blame him none."

Claire squints and leans forward. "Do you think he really believes he's a . . . wizard?"

"I can't rightly say what he's thinking. I figure he mostly believes it, or at least he figures he was one for a time. I mean, he's got all manner of stories about this or that wizardly act. If he ain't out traveling between Jupiter and the Milky Way, he's making electrical power out of citrus fruit and such as that."

"Lemons," she says, more to herself than to her guest.

"Pardon?"

"He's hung on to more than his initials."

"Ma'am?"

"Nothing," she says and her eyes fill with tears.

Cautiously, he takes a step toward her. "Are you going to be okay?"

For a few seconds Claire is too tangled up in her thoughts to speak. Finally, she sniffles and says, "I'll be fine, thanks. Thank you." She wipes her eyes. "But I want to know about all of it, the visions and the delusions. I want to know everything he's said, everything you can remember."

"Mind you, I didn't take no kind of notes or nothing, but I'll do my best if that's what you'd want."

"Please. Sit down and let me pour you some coffee."

Without waiting for an answer, Claire pours them each a cup of coffee and places a plate of cookies, cheese, and crackers in front of her guest. "Can I get you anything else?"

"No," he says. He takes a cookie in his hand, inspects it. "This'll be a mite more than I'm used to eating this time of day. Truth is, I can't recall the last time . . . But I guess that ain't exactly what you're waiting to hear about." He takes a bite of the cookie and sips his coffee before continuing.

"Now old Sam's said a whole lot of stuff, and I ain't always listened real close, cause in all actuality it can sometime get a little spooky sharing close quarters with somebody thinks he's a magician or such as that. I just sort of blocked him out when I started getting a headache or feeling queasy. Of course, I do recollect some of the stuff he said.

"Like I already told you, there was a lot of yammer about hopping around this or that planet and the like. But he could also rattle on a goodly while about his magical powers and bloody battles and shooting stars and all manner of foolishness without stopping to take more than a quick breath in between. Now, there was also a fair share of gobbledygook about kings and queens and gods and goddesses and nymphos and children clinging to his flappy raiments and whatnot in there too, but I don't quite see how you're gone be able to make a whole lot of sense out of that."

He pauses for a moment to take another bite of his cookie. "I sure wish I could give you more in the way of particulars, Ma'am, but I never did figure on having any reason to repeat any of his ramblings to a live audience. And I was sort of careful not to take him too serious and get my own brain all scrambled up in the process."

"Take your time. I want to hear all of it," Claire says. "Anything you can think of, anything you remember, no matter how trivial it might seem." She backs her chair away from the table. "But if you don't mind, I think I'd like to look in on him for a minute first."

With an involuntary groan, Chick rises. "I could go ahead and check on him for you . . . I mean if you'd want—"

"No," she says, and steers her chair toward the doorway. "You sit down and eat some more. I'd really like to have another look at him. I've waited far too long."

Left alone in the room, Chick looks around him. However different it may appear, this is the same kitchen he skulked through years before. This is the same house, the same man, this is the woman the frightened little girl at the top of the stairs has become—aside from himself, probably all that remains of that night. Certainly more than he ever would have allowed himself to imagine, but still, so much less than there would be if he and his friends had chosen some other house, or no house at all.

His stomach rumbles. He picks up another cookie, examines it and then sets it back down on his plate.

◆ ◆ ◆

"I want you both to stay here with me," Claire says to Chick a few minutes later. She's steering her chair through the kitchen doorway.

He turns to look back at her. "Oh, no, Ma'am. I mean, sure, Sam . . . or rather, your father would most likely be better off staying here with you now than out running around with me, but I figure I'll just head on out now that—"

"You don't understand," she interrupts. "I need you here. You know more about him than I do. And from what you've told me it sounds as though he considers you a . . . a friend. For all I know you may be the only friend he's had since he ran . . . since he left." She wheels her chair closer to him. "He needs you."

"It ain't right, Ma'am, me taking up space here. I figure you're going to have more than your share of trouble just having one extra person running around your house, much less two of us. Plus which you won't need no kind of distractions when you're trying to someway get through to him"—he motions to the living room—"I mean to say, if that's what you're planning to do, tell him who you are and all. It just don't feel right to me . . . staying on here I mean."

Claire reaches out and grasps his wrist. "Please don't make me beg you."

As he looks down at her hand he wants to pull back, but despite his memories, or perhaps because of them, he can't bring himself to draw his arm away.

"Well, I guess I could maybe hang around here for a day or two . . . that is if you're completely sure you'd want me to. Truth of it is, there ain't much I gotta worry about being late for."

"Thanks," she says. She gives his wrist a gentle squeeze before withdrawing her hand. "Now, I'd really appreciate it if you could help me organize the house a little. I'd like to put my father in my old bedroom upstairs. And you can have the couch . . . if that's all right with you."

His throat constricts, but he swallows dryly and says, "I'm afraid that's a damn sight better'n what I been used to."

Claire grimaces.

"I didn't mean . . . Truth is, it's not as bad as what you'd might probably think . . . Out there I mean." He rises from his chair and notices his knees are trembling. "Well, if you just tell me what you'd want me to do, I guess I'll go ahead and get started on it."

While her father remains silent and still on her living room couch, Claire escorts Chick around her house, and after instructing him on how to arrange for their stay, she wheels herself back to the kitchen. Although she wasn't prepared for guests, there is always an ample supply of food in her cabinets and refrigerator.

Less than an hour later, nervous and impatient, Claire goes into the living room to waken her father.

"I've made you some dinner." She squeezes his bony shoulder and then watches as he gradually peels his eyes open.

"I'm afraid I've been unforgivably rude."

Claire smiles.

"I'm sorry. I hadn't intended to sleep." He struggles to sit up straight.

"No. I'm glad you were able to sleep. I'm sure you needed it. Now come along and get some dinner."

"May I ask you something?"

"Of course. Anything at all."

Sam assesses the woman in the wheelchair. "I don't understand why you are being so kind to me . . . to us, two unkempt strangers you found loitering on your doorstep dressed in ill-fitting clothing. Why aren't you frightened of us, or simply disgusted, as most people would be?"

What she wants more than anything is to tell him that she's his daughter. She wants to tell him that she loves him, that she needs him, and that she always has.

"For some reason I already feel as though I know you," is what she says as she steers her chair toward the dining room. "Now come and eat."

For a few wordless minutes the three sit at the kitchen table eating the dinner Claire has prepared. Finally, Chick sets his fork on his plate and says, "This here's even better than what they was feeding us in the hospital, if you don't mind my mentioning it."

Though she makes an effort, Claire is unable to subdue a grin. "Thanks, Chick. I'll take that as a compliment."

"Oh, it sure is, Ma'am," he says, and wipes the corners of his mouth with the back of one hand.

"I'd really like you both to call me Claire."

"Yes, Ma'am," Chick says and skewers a tangled mass of noodles.

"I still don't understand what it was that brought us here, to your home," Sam says a moment later. "I am deeply confused and it troubles me. If this is the house, where are those I came to rescue, and why is it changed so? And if it is not the house, aren't we simply wasting time?"

"Of course I don't know much about this sort of thing. I mean this is all new to me, but is it possible that your dreams . . . or visions . . . do you think it's possible that whatever you've seen could just be a symbol of some kind, or maybe . . . I don't know, maybe it's something that's already happened?"

"But if it's already occurred, why should I be summoned at all?"

"I . . . I don't know. Maybe somebody . . . maybe someone still needs your help. Maybe you're here to help the survivors."

"But if it happened here, in this house, wouldn't you know something of it?"

"Well . . . It could have happened a long time ago, couldn't it? Before I . . . before I moved in."

After forcing down a mouthful of food, Chick chimes in. "Course then, I guess it could maybe be some kind of screw-up with your old wizard spells or such as that. What I mean to say is, you even said yourself how your old powers was on the decrease. I don't mean you no offense, buddy, but maybe it's just some sort of misfire in your head wiring or something, like you need a new set of spark plugs or a better grade of fuel in the old brainpan, so to say." He's so nervous and uncomfortable here, in this house, with the two of them, that he seems unable to restrain himself from babbling. "Then too, it could be it's just a optical illusion or the like." He turns toward Claire, glues his eyes to hers. "Truth of it is, I imagine there's some things you'd might be better off not knowing anyways. I mean if there ain't nothing you can do about a thing, what's the point of having the bad news?"

"You may be right, Chick," Claire says, and then turns toward her father again. "But I have a feeling there's a reason why you two have come here, to me and to this house. I've already spoken to Chick about this, Sam, and he's agreed. I'd like you two to stay here with me for a while."

Sam opens his mouth to protest, but his daughter interrupts him. "You have to stay *some*where, and I have more than enough room here for the two of you. And this house does appear to have some kind of . . . of significance."

"But—"

"My life hasn't been very interesting lately and this is . . . it's fascinating to me. Why don't we just try it for a couple days and see how it goes. Please."

Sam appraises the faintly familiar face of the woman who's so readily offered her home to two homeless strangers. There is something in her eyes, a promise or a warning. He shudders and quickly looks away.

"Okay," he says, disoriented by his own response.

◆ ◆ ◆

The following morning Claire wakens early. After telephoning a substitute teacher to cover her class for the day, she searches the phone book for a number she hasn't dialed in many years. A minute later she's speaking with the therapist who for more than ten years worked to help her deal with the incident that cut short her childhood.

"I'm sorry to bother you so early, Jill, but I just didn't know who else to call."

"What is it, Claire? What's wrong?"

"Well, my father has . . . reappeared."

"Oh my God, Claire! Are you sure it's him?"

"Of course I'm sure."

"I'm sorry. I . . . What happened? How is he? How are *you*?"

"I don't really know. I mean, he's . . . I guess he's found his own way to cope with what happened. He appears to believe, to think he's . . . someone else." She sighs. "Some kind of wizard or something. As far as I can tell he still doesn't remember anything that happened. He doesn't seem to recognize me, or the house. In fact he's apparently been having dreams or visions about that night, the night . . ."

"Yes, Claire, I know what night you mean."

"He thinks it's still going to happen, but . . . but to someone else. And he's convinced he's been sent here to stop it. I can't believe I'm even saying this. It all sounds so fucking bizarre."

"Well, I think it's interesting that he would choose to see himself as a wizard."

"Choose?"

"Well . . . not consciously, of course. But I can't help but believe there's a reason his mind went in that particular direction. Wizards are theoretically omniscient, aren't they?"

"I don't know . . . I *guess* so."

"And yet he says he knows nothing, or at least he remembers nothing. I just think there might be something more to it than meets the eye."

GRANT JARRETT   171

Suddenly, Claire recalls the game they sometimes played when she was young. "I know you always like to look for the deeper meaning, Jill," she says, "but I have a feeling it isn't quite that mysterious. Timmy and I used to love that old TV show *Mr. Wizard*, and my father always enjoyed finding entertaining ways to teach us about things. So sometimes, as a kind of treat, I guess, when we were especially well-behaved, or when he was just in a good mood, he would perform his own *Mr. Wizard* routine for us, with a makeshift cape and a cardboard hat Mom made."

"Well, you may be right. Maybe it is just that simple, though I don't really think that's any less interesting. And it may be a combination of any number of things."

Claire smiles to herself. "He used to really get into character."

"Well, that is *very* interesting. Is he lucid? Can he carry on a conversation? Aside from this wizard business, does he seem to be thinking rationally?"

"I *think* so. I mean, he's been living on the street, at least for a while, and that can't be very good for a person's mental health. But on the other hand he can communicate very well, and he at least *seems* to understand what's going on around him. It's as though someone just cut out his past and replaced it with this . . . this *other* thing. Now, I suppose, this is who he is. It's just so god-damned frustrating, after being without him for all these years, having him here, but not really having him at all."

"How did he ever find you? I mean if he says he doesn't remember anything."

"I don't know the whole story yet, but he has this friend, this guy who's been helping him, or says he has. This other guy, Chick he calls himself, is another mysterious and rather bizarre character. I don't know how, and it doesn't quite make sense, but he seems to be the one who actually located me."

"I don't understand."

"I don't either, Jill, and there is something very odd about it. I recognize that, but he's here and I don't want to scare either one of them away, so I'm not asking a lot of questions at this point. I hardly slept at all last night for fear they'd sneak out and I'd be without him again. I actually got out of bed and peeked in on him several times to assure myself he was really there. It just doesn't feel real."

"I'm sure it doesn't," Jill says. "Would you like to come in and see me? I could make time later this morning, or we could meet over my lunch hour if that's better for you."

"Well . . . maybe, I mean . . . I'm sure it wouldn't do me any harm." She laughs. "But I was thinking more about *him*. I was hoping you could see him, or recommend someone else if you're not comfortable with doing that."

"What exactly are you looking for Claire? What is it that you want?"

"I want him *back*." Her eyes fill with tears. "What *else* would I want?"

"Why don't you come in this afternoon? Can you make the time?"

"Can I bring him with me . . . if he'll come?"

"No, Claire. I think we need to talk about what it is you want, or what you expect. It's not going to be as easy as—"

"I don't expect it to be *easy*, Jill. I'm willing to do whatever it takes."

"Are you sure?"

"Of course I'm sure."

"What if what it takes is to destroy him completely?"

"What the hell is that supposed to mean?"

"His mind has invented this other world for a reason, Claire. It sounds to me as though it has protected him for a very long time from what happened, from having to face reality. If you attempt to bring him back to . . . to your world, to what you and I call reality, you could risk losing him completely. And I know you don't want that."

"Don't you think he'd want to have his own daughter back in his life?"

"Of course he would. I'm sure he would if he had any say in the matter, and if it didn't come at such a terrible cost. But if you try to strip away the fantasy that's been shielding him from the truth, there's no way of knowing what will happen. His condition could very easily worsen. My guess is that his mind did what it *had* to do to avoid a total shutdown. Obviously, I don't have a lot of firsthand information about his case, and this is more than a little out of my realm, but I know as well as you do what happened to him, to all of you, and I can assure you that trying to bring him back could, at least in theory, cost him whatever sanity he has. It could destroy what's left of him. And there is no guarantee that you could break through his defenses anyway. As ridiculous as it might sound to you and me, this wizard thing *is* his reality now. It's most likely all he knows. Of course, there are different theories about these kinds of situations, about just about everything psychological, but I think the general consensus among reputable experts based on the little we know would be to let him be after all this time, that he is where he *needs* to be to continue to survive."

"But . . . I just can't stand the thought, the idea that I can't comfort him, and that he can't comfort *me*. It just isn't fair."

"No, it's *not* fair. But you're hoping that you'll be able to get through to him and he'll suddenly be your sweet, loving father again. I just don't think that's a very realistic expectation."

"But *I* got through it, and *I* was just a child. Why the hell can't *he*? It's been thirty fucking years."

"We've been through all of this, Claire. People react differently. You can't be in his head and you've told me yourself that you don't know exactly what happened that night. You simply cannot know what another human being has been through. Yes, you were young at the time, but your youth may have worked in your favor. It almost certainly did. But my sense is that this isn't what you want to hear right now."

"What I want to hear, Jill, is that you can help me, and that you can help my father—"

"I'd be willing to consider talking with him *after* you and I get together . . . *if* he's willing. But I must caution you, based on what you've told me, I don't think anyone is going to benefit from an effort to somehow revive his memory. I'm sorry, but I don't think that's the kind of risk either one of us is going to be willing to take. I know how you must feel, Claire, being so close to him after so long without really being able to . . . to embrace him, but I also know you would never forgive yourself if in an effort to reclaim him you did further harm."

"What he has now isn't really a life. How much worse could he be?"

"He doesn't sound tortured right now. That could very easily change. He could become severely psychotic, he could certainly become suicidal."

"But he's here now, and I want him. I need him, for God's sake."

"I *know* you do, but—"

"There must be drugs that help with this kind of thing. Don't you have medications for this stuff?"

"What are you going to do? Are you going to slip him a lithium and clozapine cocktail every night before you tuck him in? I'm sorry, Claire, but you really need to come in and see me. You can't expect to handle this kind of thing alone."

"No! No, Jill. I've been through all of that. I've dealt with my goddamned feelings and talked and talked till there's nothing more to say and I'm still a wreck." She presses her eyelids shut. "I'm going to go now, Jill. Thanks very much for your advice. Really." She places the receiver gently in its cradle and wipes the tears from her face. When the phone rings seconds later, she doesn't bother to pick it up.

◆ ◆ ◆

As she glides slowly down the stair lift, Claire notices Chick sitting alone on the couch. His hands are clenched together as if in prayer, his eyes tightly shut.

"Are you okay?" she asks, and releases her wheelchair from the lift.

"Oh." He rubs his eyes. "Morning, miss. Truth is, I was just now waking up."

"I'm sorry. Did you sleep okay?"

"I slept some, I guess you could say."

"Was it too cold?"

"Oh, no, Ma'am. I'm used to . . . It was just about right for me. Maybe I just wasn't quite so tired as what I figured."

She nods. "Does my . . . Does he usually sleep this late?"

"Fact of it is, we don't much abide by any kind of usually. We pretty much sleep and eat whenever the situation allows. I imagine old Sam's got a lot of both to make up for, same as me, but it might take more than a little adjusting for him to get back to what you'd call a normal-type schedule."

"Would you like some breakfast?"

"I think I'd like to cook up something for *you* if that'd be okay . . . I mean if you'd be willing to trust me banging around in your kitchen there."

"You don't need to do that."

"It's been quite a while now, but I done some work here and there as a short order cook in a couple of greasy spoon type of places. I know that ain't much of a résumé to speak of but I guess I can fry up a pretty decent egg if you got any. And it'd make me feel a mite better about eating your food if you'd let me work a little for it."

"All right. But I think I'd like to wait for . . . for Sam."

"I wouldn't worry too much about that, Ma'am. He'll be up and around once he gets a whiff of some hot food. If you don't mind, I'll just make up my bed here, and then I'll go ahead and see if I can make my way around your kitchen without doing too much damage. Just kind of get things started anyways."

Claire nods and wheels herself toward the dining room, but before she is through the broad doorway, Chick calls out to her.

"Ma'am?"

"Yes?" she says, and stops.

"Pardon my inquiring, but did they ever catch up with them guys who killed your mom?"

"My mom *and* my brother." She turns her head to scrutinize her guest. "Yes, as a matter of fact, they did."

"Did they get tried and all?"

"They were both killed in a shootout with the police."

For a moment Chick just stands there. Finally, he says, "Did it help any . . . I mean does it make you feel a little better knowing they got . . . took care of?"

"I don't know. I'm certainly glad they weren't able to hurt anyone else, but beyond that, I really don't know." She pinches the bridge of her nose and says, "I'll get the kitchen in order for you."

Chick watches her glide through the dining room and into the kitchen. "I'm sorry, Ma'am," he says, too softly for her to hear.

Twenty minutes later, Claire sits at the table watching while Chick prepares scrambled eggs and toast for the three of them. She thinks about the kitchen help at the school where she teaches, and about the custodial staff. Her father's case is clear enough; his future was torn from him along with his wife and son. But how did this man—a man who at least seems decent and honest, a man who appears to care about those around him and to want to work for what he's given—how did he become mired in this hopeless life he's living? He's a little crude and apparently uneducated, but he doesn't seem stupid, slow, or lazy.

"Chick?" she says, when she hears her father stirring upstairs. "I don't want to offend you, and you certainly don't have to answer me if you don't want to, but I'd like to ask you something."

He turns his back to the stove. "I guess that's fair enough, Ma'am."

"How did you wind up . . . living on the street? What I'm asking is, do you have a drinking problem, or was it drugs, or, well . . . I think you know what I'm getting at."

"I suppose I do. Near as I can tell, it's just sort of what I was made for, being out on the street I mean. Kind of like my own special calling, I guess you could say."

Claire continues to watch him as he turns back to the stove. A few minutes later Sam is standing in the doorway.

"Come on in." Claire motions to an empty chair. "Join the party."

"I'm sorry, but now that we're here my impatience is only growing," Sam says. He lowers himself slowly into the seat. "I must have wakened more than a dozen times last night to images of violence and death."

"Would you mind if I asked you a few questions?"

"Of course not."

"You say you've seen this woman's face." Although Claire can still hear her therapist's admonitions, she's not yet willing to give up hope.

"Yes, though only for seconds at a time."

"And you said she and I look . . . similar."

He closes his eyes for a moment. Though the image he conjures isn't clear, and it fades almost as swiftly as it came, the similarities are there. "Yes, there is a resemblance."

"Does that mean anything to you?"

"It gives me some hope that in spite of the contradictory evidence, we've come to the right place, that this may not be a waste of time."

"Does the name Stephen—"

"Grub's ready," Chick interrupts her. "Better scarf it up while it's good and hot." With a noisy flurry of activity he places three full plates on the table and takes a seat.

"Thanks so much, Chick," Claire says, and smiles. "This looks great." She turns back to her father. "Do you get any feelings when I say the name—"

"I hope you like your eggs scrambled, Ma'am," Chick interrupts again. "I should of asked, but that's a mite easier than trying to cook them over easy, for *me* anyways." He glances at Sam and then back at Claire. "You never know when they're going to up and break on you, do you, Ma'am?"

"Merciful heavens, let the poor woman speak," Sam says. "What is the name?"

Claire can feel Chick glaring at her now, and though she's uncertain about the wisdom of what she's about to do, she keeps her eyes trained on her father. "Does the name Stephen Mallory mean anything at all to you?"

Sam places his fork on his plate and takes a deep breath. "Mallory is your own name."

"Yes, it is."

"I'm afraid there are no names in my visions. I don't know who the people are, I only know they seem to be in grave danger."

Chick releases a raspy sigh, but Claire forges on.

"But is the name Stephen Mallory . . . is it familiar? Have you ever heard it before?"

Sam lets his eyes fall shut. Suddenly, the room seems to be swaying, teetering. With his right hand he grasps the edge of the table, and for a minute he grips it so tightly his fingers ache. When the dizzying motion has finally subsided, he opens his eyes and says, "It means nothing to me. Nothing at all. I'm sorry."

"All right then," Chick says. "I guess that's the end of that. So how's your eggs, Sam?"

"As palatable as any eggs I've eaten in years, which is to say they are actually warm and fresh. But I'm feeling a little unwell." He turns to Claire. "I'm sorry, but would you mind if I were to excuse myself?"

"Of course not," Claire says. "Are you okay?"

"Just a little weary from the journey I suppose."

"Why don't you go upstairs and lie down for a while, and let me know if you need anything."

Still dizzy, Sam rises. "Thank you," he says, and looks over at his friend. "The breakfast is good. I'm just feeling a little shaky, and my back has begun to throb again."

When she can hear her father stirring upstairs, Claire leans toward Chick. "Why don't you want him to know?"

"It ain't quite exactly that, Ma'am. It's just I'm kind of afraid of what might happen if he starts remembering now."

"Sounds like you've been talking to Jill."

"Pardon?"

"My therapist."

"Oh . . . no, Ma'am. I wouldn't know nothing about that."

"What makes you think he couldn't adjust? Don't you think he'd want to know who I am? Don't you think he'd want to have a relationship with his own daughter after all these years alone?"

Chick scrutinizes the woman. There is one detail about that night from which she's apparently been spared. Maybe if she knew the truth about how her brother died, maybe then she would understand. Maybe then she would allow her father to remain where he is, in his own world, protected by his own unwillingness or inability to know the truth. But disclosing what he knows would implicate Chick in the crime, in the slaughter. Claire would despise him, probably have him arrested, and if Sam found out, he too would hate him. And though he couldn't blame them, it would be, for him, for Chick, such a devastating loss.

He thinks about his friend, about the distant past, and he looks again at the daughter who's somehow survived. Maybe, if he had a better life, more to lose, he would resist the urge to tell her. But he has so little to lose and this debt is so long overdue. Finally Chick clears his throat.

"I got something to tell you, Ma'am," he says. "And . . . and it ain't pretty at all, and you ain't going to think too highly of me after I tell it neither, but I don't figure how I got much choice now, and truth is I'm just awful damn tired of putting it off. So I'd appreciate it if you just let me have my say and then do whatever it is you figure you gotta do."

Claire can see her guest's pale hands trembling, wrestling with one another, and though she isn't certain why, she can feel her own heart slapping at her chest. "Do you know something . . . something more?"

"Yes, Ma'am."

"Well for God's sake, *talk* to me."

"First off, I'd want you to know I wouldn't do no harm to neither one of you. What I'm saying is, in the past I done some things would give you reason to fret, but I'd rather get my damn head run over by a farm tractor than hurt either one of you, or anybody else for that matter."

"I'm not so sure I trust my instincts about anything at this point, Chick, but I . . . I have a feeling that's probably true."

"I could sure as hell use a drink, Ma'am. And a cigarette too."

"I don't drink, and I do very little entertaining. I've never been able to stand the smell of cigarette smoke. I'm sorry, but I'm afraid I can't help you out with either one at the moment."

"I sort of hate to press the issue, Ma'am, but are you sure you ain't maybe got a bottle of something set aside for special occasions or the like? It don't need to be nothing special. Just something to loosen me up a touch."

She shakes her head. "I'm sorry."

"I guess I'll get right to it then." He pauses to wait for a response, but Claire says nothing.

"Well, as it so happens, old Sam seen something you don't likely know about that night. I mean, maybe you might of seen it too and just don't remember seeing it, or maybe you was lucky enough to somehow miss it altogether, but as far as I can tell it's the worse part of the whole damn nightmare, and you know that's saying something. And I got a pretty good idea it might of been the thing what put him over the line, so to say. I mean, maybe if it didn't happen he'd of been able to go on with his life just like what it sort of looks like you done."

Chick's heart is racing now, and though his face is glazed with perspiration, he feels cold and faint. Still, it's too late now to stop.

"When your father come down the stairs with his gun, your mom . . . well she was already dead, Ma'am, and one of them two guys the cops shot was holding that damn knife to that little boy's . . . to your brother's throat. For a minute there it was a sort of standoff, but when your dad finally got a gander at your mom laid out on the floor . . . I guess he kind of lost his balance, so to say. Well, that's when the guy what was holding your brother tosses him aside and real quick lunges at your dad with his knife." Chick scowls down at his own hands. "I'm sorry, Ma'am." He swallows dryly and clears his throat. "When your brother seen the guy start toward your dad, I guess he tried to jump in and somehow stop him, to protect his . . . your dad, but Sam, he didn't expect the little fella to come toward him, and so when he goes to shoot the guy . . . when he goes to pull the trigger, the little boy . . . well, he gets hisself right in the way . . . in the way of the shot. Ma'am, there wasn't nothing he could of did different. He couldn't of knowed what was going to happen. The two of them was trying to save each other and it just got all tangled up. He couldn't of did nothing different than what he done. Couldn't of . . ."

Claire sits silently staring at nothing. Like cars colliding on a foggy freeway, her thoughts stack up while she tries to digest what she's just heard. For a moment everything stalls and there is a sort of mental gridlock. Then suddenly she feels as though she's falling again, sinking deeper and deeper into some cold, formless void. She tries to focus on Chick, but gradually the inky shapes swirling on the edges of her vision begin to close in on his frowning face. She hears herself say something and soon there is nothing but darkness and distant echoes. And then there is nothing at all.

◆ ◆ ◆

When she peels her eyes open again, Claire is in her living room. There is a blanket draped over her and a pillow has been wedged between her head and the wall behind her. Across from her on the couch Chick sits staring at her, his hands folded tightly on his lap.

"I didn't know what else to do with you, Ma'am. I checked a couple of times, and you was breathing pretty good, so I just figured you was going to wake up soon enough. I didn't—"

"I'm assuming . . ." With her eyes Claire motions upward. "I assume he didn't tell you all of that. I mean, if *he* doesn't know what you told me, well . . ."

"No, Ma'am, he don't know none of it. I'm afraid them two

guys what broke in that night wasn't alone . . . But I didn't expect nobody to get hurt. And I didn't hurt nobody, I swear that to you, Ma'am. But I was right here when it happened and no two ways about it, and I guess I didn't do nothing to stop it. I mean to say I *know* I didn't. I was with them. I would of liked to of stopped them, but it was just too much for me. It was all crazy and I was young and no good for nothing. No good at all."

"I need some water."

"I'd like to get it for you if that's okay."

Claire shrugs and turns away.

◆ ◆ ◆

While the water swirls down the drain, Chick stands bending over the squat kitchen sink pondering what remains of his future. There's little more he can do for Sam now, or for his daughter. He's returned the man to his home and to his daughter, and he's finally confessed his part in the crime. It isn't much—maybe it's nothing at all, but it's the only thing he could think to do. And though he feels no relief from the guilt he's been carrying, he's convinced now that he never will. He's not particularly surprised to learn that for him there will be no redemption, just disappointed, and wearier now than he's been in all the years during which he's been running.

But what now? He could sneak out the back door, the same door through which he entered that night, and run, run again. He could keep running until his legs give out, or his lungs, or his heart. What difference would it make to anyone? He could take the same route he took the last time he fled from this house and just keep going until he drops or gets shot or run over. What would it change? Nothing he does will make any difference now. Except for that one time, the time he failed so horribly, it never has, and he knows now that it never will.

A voice somewhere inside him shouts *run,* and then it shouts again, louder this time, closer, more strident, more desperate. And then the voice screams so loud that he's afraid his skull will shatter:

run! He steps toward the door and stops himself and the voice cries out again. *Run, you idiot. Run!* His body trembling, he takes another step and reaches out toward the door. He sees the woman and the child, and he sees his friend and like a crack of thunder the voice screams out again, *Run!* He thinks of his entire life, a precious gift—he's heard it called that somewhere—wasted, tossed away because of weakness and fear, and somehow he chokes the voice back down, cursing himself for wanting to leave, for staying, for his weakness, for being alive. He fills a tall glass with water, turns off the faucet, and returns to the living room.

◆ ◆ ◆

"Why?" Claire says coldly, after devouring the water.

"I was just a stupid kid. I never would of figured anything like . . . like what happened could happen. These guys was bad, but not like . . . never nothing like that."

"No. That's not what I mean. Why did you come back here? Why did you bring him back? It makes no sense."

"No, I don't guess it does."

"So why don't you explain it to me?"

"Well, we just sort of got to be friends. I didn't have no idea who he was at first, so when he started talking about his visions and all, I didn't know what in the hell was going on. Truth is, he had me spooked for a while there, talking about something no one else should of knowed about. You see . . . well I thought *he* was dead too. Sure as hell looked like it when I skipped out."

"Skipped out?"

"Yes, Ma'am. I run away that night. That's how come I'm still alive I guess. Anyways, when he kept going on and things got to sound more familiar I thought maybe it was some kind of signal or something like that, like somebody, I don't know, maybe God if there is one . . . maybe God or somebody was trying for some reason to tell me to come back here and face up to what we done. See, I never once come anywheres near here after it happened. I couldn't stand the thought of it. But then, when I seen the scar and realized who he was, and he was still alive and all, I figured maybe I could somehow do something right for once."

"You're just a saint, aren't you?"

"No, Ma'am. I guess you know good and well I ain't no saint. I just wanted to sort of try and make up for some of what I done to him and his . . . and you. Course then, when we started getting closer, I got to wondering wasn't the whole damn thing just another one of my bad ideas."

"When you started to realize you might get caught and punished?"

"Well, not exactly, leastwise that wasn't the main thing. More like I begun to figure maybe he'd be better off not knowing no more than he already did. And plus which, I didn't much want to take the chance of losing him . . . losing him as a friend, Ma'am."

"So then . . . if that's true, what was it that finally persuaded you to bring him here?"

"Ma'am . . . unfortunately, I ain't never been much good at figuring what the right thing is. I mean, if I decide on doing a particular thing, and I'm dumb enough to go ahead and do it, it's a pretty fair bet I'll soon come to learn that's just the exact thing I shouldn't of did. I guess that's one of the reasons I ain't done one hell of a lot for most of my life. Then too, once old Sam . . . I mean to say, once your father got his mind latched onto the idea of finding the guy he thought he was seeing in his visions, I couldn't hardly do nothing to talk him out of it. Truth is, for a minute or two there, I give some serious consideration to the idea of leading him astray and putting the whole thing behind the both of us, but . . . but then I seen you, in that there wheelchair, and it was too much for me. I just sort of give up trying to figure it out.

"I still ain't sure did I do wrong or right bringing him here, Ma'am. Fact of it is, I'm more than a little worried about him now, what with his getting sick or whatever it was was happening to him at the table. I mean, he ain't never looked all that healthy since the first time I seen him, but when he started turning all green and sickly looking there, I got a bad feeling."

"Did you kill my mother, Chick? Or whatever your name is."

"No, Ma'am. I swear to you—"

"Did you murder my brother?" She tightens her hands into fists.

"No, all I did was . . . I just stood there like a—"

"Did you hurt my father? Were you the one who cut his throat?"

"No, Ma'am, I swear it. And I ain't never forgave myself for . . ."

It takes another minute for the eruption to come. But when it comes, Claire's voice is deep, feral. "How dare you come into my house?" she snarls, her hands gripping her own lifeless knees. "How *dare* you come into my home and act like you're my friend . . . like, like you want to *help* me, like you want to *help* my father." Even she doesn't recognize this new voice, a voice that speaks for the years of anger that have been festering inside her. "Even if part of what you say is true, you're no better than your . . . than your friends. You're an evil, murdering son of a bitch." She takes a deep breath to calm herself. "I don't care what you did or didn't do. You're every bit as guilty as they are."

He stares down at the floor. "I know it, Ma'am."

Neither of them has noticed Sam making his way quietly down the stairs. But when he speaks they can both hear the distress in his voice. "Why do you assail my friend?"

"I . . ." Claire's throat tightens.

"She ain't assailin' me, Sam. We was just having a sort of a serious discussion."

"Actually, I was just about to ask your friend to leave, or maybe get him an escort."

"I don't understand."

Despite her concerns for her father, Claire is unable now to control the rage that's been churning inside her. "Your friend was just confessing to his criminal past. It seems he's got quite a colorful history. Were you aware of that?"

"No, I wasn't," Sam says, and continues down the stairs. "I've never bothered to inquire. I'm sure there is much about Chick that I don't know, but his past matters little to me. I've come to trust him, to care for him. Whatever might be in his past, he is a true and . . . and a very dear friend to me."

"Really? Is that what you think?"

"Ma'am." Chick isn't certain now who he is protecting, or from what. He only knows that it feels wrong to reveal to Sam what he has shared with his daughter. "Ma'am," he continues. "You can do whatever you want with me. I don't much care about that, but I'm not sure it's such a good idea to go into any kind of detail right now with—"

"Do you really expect me to take *your* advice?"

"No, Ma'am, I don't guess I do, but I think you should think real careful about your f . . . about Sam . . . I mean about helping him do what he come here for. Please, Ma'am. I can leave right now, or you can call the—"

"No." Sam's tone is firm. "I respect that this is your home, but I won't let my friend depart without me. You have been more than kind to me, to us both, but if you banish him from your home, you also banish me. In all my long, lonely years as a mortal, no one I can recall has treated me better than this man. I've trusted no one more, and never once, never once has he disappointed me."

Claire feels the walls closing in on her. The choice, in this impossible moment, is to relinquish her father after waiting a lifetime to reclaim him, or to share her home with one of the men who took him from her. Risk her own life and her father's, or let him go yet again, and spend the rest of her life wondering if she could have done more, if she could have salvaged something from the wreckage. An unthinkable choice.

No choice at all.

"No," she says, and for a split second she sees herself dead in her bed, her own throat slit. "You can both . . . you can both stay. It was nothing. Just a misunderstanding." She looks up at her father. "I'm sorry." She forces a weak smile and her stomach clenches. "Are you feeling any better?"

"I don't know what happened to me earlier, but yes, much better. Actually, it seems my appetite has returned, though my back still feels as though it were trapped in some giant vise."

"How about if I cook something else up for you?" Chick offers. "I mean if that'd be okay with you, Ma'am."

"I'll do it," she says without glancing at him.

"I still don't know," Sam says, and sighs.

"What is it?" Claire asks.

"It just isn't proper . . . your feeding us, giving us a place to sleep. I've done some begging, and I've even resorted to more shameful acts in order to survive, but this, living in your home, eating your food . . . It isn't . . . it simply doesn't feel right."

Claire fixes her eyes on his. "It's been a long time, a very long time since I dared to entertain the thought that things happen for a reason—since I was a child, I guess. And to be honest, I'm still not sure I'm willing to open my mind to that possibility. Frankly, I'm not sure it's wise . . . or healthy. But your being here is . . . it means something to me. I can't explain it to you, at least not yet, but I want you here. I *need* you here.

"I suppose you think I'm just a lonely, desperate cripple, or maybe that I'm crazy, and I really wouldn't blame you if you did, but . . . but that's not it." She glances at Chick. "At least I don't believe it is," she says before wheeling herself through the dining room and into the kitchen.

When he can see that Claire is occupied in the kitchen, Chick turns to Sam and says, "I think it's just about time for me to head on out, Sam. I mean . . . I figure the two of us has gone about as far as we can together, and you'd most likely be better off staying here and doing whatever it is you figure you gotta do."

"You are my friend, Chick, the only friend I've had for . . . for countless years."

"Well, I'm thinking you got yourself a new friend now, and one what'll most likely be able to take better care of you . . . I mean to say, I expect you'd be better off here, what with the cold weather and your back acting up and all. Like she said, I figure there's a reason why you come out here. I just sort of tagged along. Fact of it is I'm a mite younger than you, and truth to be told, I'm starting to get kind of fidgety, holed up here in this big old house with nothing to do but twiddle my thumbs."

"From what I've been able to gather you've always been honest with me. It would disappoint me were that to change now, after we've come so far. I can see well enough that you are troubled. If I can help in some way—"

"Oh, no. You done way more than enough for me already."

"Maybe this is all a mistake," Sam says, and motions to the walls around them. "Maybe the visions have misdirected me, misdirected us both. If you are ill at ease, we can depart, we can move on together. We can leave right now, today. I won't deny that there is a sense of safety and comfort here, with the food, the warm bed, the shelter from the bitter wind, but there is also an ominous undercurrent, some nebulous menace lurking just out of view, and I don't like to admit it, but it . . . it frightens and disconcerts me in a way I don't understand. But even more important is all I've learned from you, Chick." He smiles. "I've learned, or maybe relearned, though I guess it's all the same, the value of honest, caring human relationships, and about the simple human joy of sharing."

Chick is stung by the statement. "Oh, I don't figure I had anything to do with all of that—"

"Yes, you did, and you've enabled me to laugh again. And you've taught me to trust, which may be the most important lesson of all."

"Come and get it," Claire calls from the kitchen.

"You better go ahead and eat." Chick tries his best to smile.

Sam assesses his friend for a moment longer before stepping out of the room.

◆ ◆ ◆

As her father eats, Claire sits across from him silently trying to make sense of the little she knows, or thinks she knows about him, and about the perplexing man who delivered him to her. There is no question now that Chick played a role in the crime that brought them all here. There was indeed a third man. And yet, he has returned and he's brought her father with him. What could his motivation possibly be? What could he expect to gain? Unless he was crazy, which didn't appear to be the case, he had to understand that there was some risk, if not from the law, then from those who haven't forgotten, from anyone who might still lust for vengeance, and now from her. Though he doesn't seem an evil man on the surface, what kind of man involves himself in acts so brutal, so vile? What kind of a man stands by and watches while an innocent family is slaughtered? Certainly not the kind of man you invite into your home. But then she didn't feel she had a choice.

"How long have you known your friend?" she asks when her father's plate is empty.

"More than a month, less than a year, I suppose. Long enough, I think, to know him."

"Does he ever talk about his past?" She peers out through the dining room into the living room. He isn't in her line of sight.

"Chick has never been particularly forthcoming about the details of his history, but then with the sort of life he seems to have led, indeed, the sort of life we've *both* led, the details may not be very telling. In fact they might be misleading."

"I don't understand," she says, and leans toward him.

"We simply survive as best we can. Where and when, and even how, to the extent that you are doing no serious harm, mean little. The truth . . . what you would likely call the truth, doesn't lie in the particulars, in the day-to-day facts. The truth is both larger and smaller than that. It is some mysterious force that resides in the heart. It is in whatever scrap of dignity you can cling to while you're scraping by. There are the simple facts, the everyday details, and then there is the story. And then there is the person. What a man is, what he truly is, transcends the momentary facts of his life, I think. We are far more than the sum of our actions.

There is what we do, and what we've done, and then there is what we are, what we truly are."

For just a second, she can hear her father's voice. No, not his voice, but certainly his words, his ideas. "I think I know what you mean, but don't you judge a man by what he's done? Don't some of his actions, his choices, characterize him? They have an impact after all."

"Among other things, I suppose. Certainly, a man's actions are the result of the choices he's made, and these acts have consequences, but just as people we would describe as evil occasionally perform acts of kindness, good people, people who are good at heart, sometimes do things that you and I might judge as reprehensible. People, even good, decent people, make mistakes, misjudgments. Weakness and ignorance are not the same as evil, are they? And even despicable people must on occasion rise above their past deeds. I think what a person is in his heart is a far more accurate gauge of who he is than the mistakes he may have made or what he may have once been. And at times we have little choice about where life carries us.

"It's true that Chick is a mendicant, and in some sense a criminal, too, I imagine, though I've never sensed the capacity for violence in him. He lacks education and refinement and he has done what he's had to do. In a way he is a testament to life's unrelenting desperation to continue, like the tiny flowers that force their way up through cracks in the city sidewalk. He's probably begged and stolen and lied and swindled and who knows what else. And so, I regret to confess, have I. But for as long as I've known him, Chick has been generous with the little bit he's had, and with his seemingly unwavering spirit. And don't let his speech and manners mislead you; he is far more intelligent, far more perceptive than he appears. He's been a caring companion, and I would trust him, indeed I *have* trusted him with my very life."

"Would you trust him with the life of . . . of a parent, or a child?"

Sam sits back in the chair and sighs. "I suppose I'll never know the answer to that, but I believe I would."

For a short time father and daughter are silent. Finally, Sam pushes his plate away and says, "Now I have a question for you. I know by now how the world works, how people think. This is what continues to baffle me. Why would you trust *me*? Why would you let either one of us into your home? I know what you've said, but to me it still makes no sense. I can find no logic in your explanation."

"Logic," she says, and smiles. "But I *do* know you, Sam. I know who you are. We share a history, a bond I can't . . . I can't yet explain. I don't know, perhaps I'll never be able to explain it to you, but it is there, and it is every bit as real to me as this wheelchair, and I think you know it too; somewhere, in some way, I think, I *hope* you know—" The words become lodged in her throat. Quickly, she turns toward the sink and starts the water running.

◆ ◆ ◆

For the next few hours, the three move quietly about the house, their hopes and fears distinct, but hopelessly entangled at the roots. After taking a long hot shower, Sam straightens up the room where he slept, the room where his children used to sleep, and then he sits on the bed and waits, though he doesn't quite know for what. Downstairs in the living room, Chick sits alone, trying to force his weight down into the padded cushions of the couch, to disappear, aware that no matter how deep he sinks he'll never be able to hide from his memories, from himself. And while the two men grapple with their own elusive ghosts, Claire sits in her bedroom, paging, expressionless, through a leather-bound photo album.

Black and white pictures fill the stained and faded pages, their corners locked in place by triangles of heavy ivory paper, worn and ragged and yellowed with age. Scattered throughout the album in no apparent pattern are photographs of the four of them, photographs of the children posing or playing together, photographs of days and events she can only vaguely imagine, the memories almost unrecognizable now, blurred by the merciless motion of time, recreated over and over and therefore suspect. There are pictures of a handsome man and his pretty wife, and in every one they look happy, proud of what they have, proud of each other. They look comfortable, invulnerable. Of course there is much that can't be seen in pictures, but she would gladly take even the worst of what they had then to reclaim just a moment of the joy they shared. She would gladly endure a thousand tense days and wordless nights for just a hint of the closeness they had.

If she showed the pictures to her father, would he know? Would it all come rushing back to him? Would he finally embrace his lost daughter or would he crumble and disintegrate like a waking dream? For thirty years she's been strong; for thirty years she's waited. She's hoped until all reason was gone and then she continued to hope. And now he is here, and still she has nothing more than hope, and precious little of that.

There he is, standing over a charcoal grill, smiling at the camera. And there again, on some washed-out beach in New Jersey with the only wife he would ever take. There is her mother on the living room floor, playing with the children, with Timmy and her, just babies, barely a year apart. There is the entire family in the backyard, maybe a year before it happened, maybe not that long. Maybe longer. What does it matter? Everyone looks so innocent, so immune to the dangers of the world outside their own, dark dangers that could never touch them. Not them.

But Claire knows now that there is no immunity, knows that the ugly world that existed only elsewhere respects no boundaries.

Later, when she knocks on the door to her father's room, Claire isn't certain what she's going to say.

"Yes?"

"Do you mind if I come in?"

"Of course not."

She pushes the door open and wheels herself in. He's sitting on the edge of the bed. "But I want you to feel at home here."

"You are still concerned about my friend."

"Yeah. I suppose I am."

"Then I'd like to tell you a story."

"Okay," she says, and steers her chair a little closer. "I'd love a story."

"On the way here, we were forced to stop and stay overnight in Indianapolis, out on the street. While we were sleeping, or attempting to sleep, we were assaulted by a pack of youths. It was terrifying, but at risk of his own life, Chick protected me from the gang."

"Well that's very nice, but wasn't he also protecting himself? And what if he thought you were worth something to him? Wouldn't he protect you if he thought you might be valuable to him?"

"I suppose so, though I can't imagine what he might expect to gain from me. But it wasn't merely the fact that he defended me. As they were attempting to flee, he ensnared one of the offenders. According to the laws of the street, most likely the only laws he knows, he had a right to do whatever harm he wished to the young man. I watched him raise over his head one of the bats they used to beat us. I watched his taut features gradually slacken as he pondered his options. I heard him say, 'I can't,' and then let the misguided youth go."

"That's a good story."

"But not enough. Then I'll tell you more. This selfsame man was angry with me for days when he thought I'd allowed a catfight to go on outside our makeshift domicile. A small thing, perhaps, but is that the behavior of a dangerous man?"

"I don't know. I don't know much of anything right now."

"Listen to your heart."

"I'm afraid my heart is a little confused these days."

"I'm sorry."

"Can I tell you something?"

"Of course. Anything you wish."

"You remind me of my father."

Sam assesses the woman in the wheelchair. "A compliment, I assume."

"Yes. It is. I lost him when I was very young."

"I am sorry."

"He was always careful not to judge people too harshly." She chuckles. "Sometimes it would make my mother angry. She thought he was too easy on people."

"Is your mother still alive?"

"I lost them both. But what about you? What were your parents like?"

"I am hundreds, maybe thousands of years old," he says, and smiles. "That part of my history is a blur, like a remote galaxy seen through aging eyes, just a faint speck I'm no longer quite certain I'm seeing. I'm afraid the details of my provenance are a mystery now, even to me."

"Please don't be offended . . . but, do you really believe you are a . . . a wizard?"

"Why wouldn't I believe it? Why shouldn't I?"

"Well, do you . . . Can you perform, I don't know . . . feats?"

"Sadly, I seem to have lost all but the most insignificant of my powers. In most ways, I suppose, I am as human now as you."

"Wouldn't you like to know about . . . about your beginnings?"

"I suppose I was formed of some random amalgam of stardust and dark matter, or perhaps I am the product of the passionate union of two gods."

"Have you ever had a . . . a loved one?"

"My one true regret is that I cannot recall with any degree of clarity the goddess I loved and the two perfect cherubs that together we spawned."

"A wife and two children?"

"That would be the mortal description."

"You know, it's funny. My father sometimes used to make believe he was a wizard. He would dress up and do scientific experiments. He would even alter the way he spoke, to try to sound lofty or formal, the way he imagined a wizard might speak, or maybe it was the way he thought *we* imagined a wizard would speak."

"The way I speak. Is that what you mean?"

"Yes. I guess it is."

"I think I know what you are intimating." He squints his eyes. "And I suppose I could alter my own speech, to sound less formal, if for some reason I needed or desired to do so. But the way I speak comes perfectly naturally to me, and it would ill befit a true wizard to sound uneducated or coarse. It is not an act or a cheap fabrication. It is not an affectation."

"What if you could see your wife again, or your children? Would you want to see them, to be with them if you could?"

"Of course." He lets his eyes fall shut. "Of course I would."

"What would you be willing to sacrifice?"

"I have little worth giving, but I would gladly give it all." He opens his eyes, fixes them on hers. "I would give whatever remains of my life."

She could tell him now, just say it and be done with it. Or she could show him the photo album and let the information sink in slowly. But if Jill is right, if the impact of the truth were to do further damage to his fragile mind, what would be gained, for either of them? And because of Chick's disclosure about her father's inadvertent role in her brother's death, she understands why he had no choice but to let go of his sanity, why he had to create his own world. How could a man who so loved his children live with that awful truth?

Though the knowledge tears at her heart, she understands now that she can never reclaim her father.

"I guess you can still remember loving them," she says.

"The memory of what we shared has helped to keep me warm and safe on my darkest days. Even today, I can feel their love."

"They're still with you, Sam," she says. "They still love you as you love them, as I continue to love the father I lost."

Sam's eyes well up with tears. "Do you really think so?" he asks.

"In my heart . . . In my heart, I know it."

"Do they know . . . Do you think they know how dearly I love them?"

"I know it. I guess I know they do."

◆ ◆ ◆

In the early morning, before the sun has risen, Sam drifts into a dream. It begins in much the same way as the others, but this time, when the stranger fires the gun, Sam sees clearly the face of the child as the bullet rips through it. He sees the awful spray of blood, tissue, and bone that showers out in all directions. Then, as though the earth has been pulled out from under him, the child slinks slowly toward the ground, and Sam hears a man scream out, a terrible wrenching wail that seems to go on forever. Then he is standing outside of the man, gazing back at him. It's gloomy in the room and the man's face is distorted with terror and grief, but Sam can see his eyes and he can see his own reflection staring back at him from those eyes. A minute passes and the man stands motionless before him, a brittle statue formed of horror and despair, his expression unchanged. Suddenly a shiny blade tears into the man's neck, ripping it open. A stream of blood pours out in slow motion, like rich red molasses. In the flowing blood are fluid images, images of a family, images of a happy life. A beautiful woman spills out in the crimson stream, her long dark hair flowing behind her, then a little boy with a wide smile, and finally a pretty little girl. The girl is waving, and her lips are moving, but he can hear no words. Then they are all gone. The blood stops flowing, and instead of falling to the ground, the man begins to age. Deep wrinkles appear, first around his eyes, then across his forehead, and finally around his mouth. Then a beard of tangled twigs begins to grow from his face and neck. Suddenly Sam sees his own face, eyes accusing, mouth open, a terrible bestial growl pouring out from within.

When he awakens, Chick is sitting next to him on the bed, grasping his shoulder and calling his name.

"You're just having a bad dream, Sam."

"No," Sam says, his voice quaking. "It wasn't a dream. It was real, and it was horrible." He begins to sob and Chick leans closer and puts his arms around him.

"It's okay, buddy. Honest, it was just a dream."

"No, Chick. It meant something, something . . . I don't know."

Chick releases his friend and sits up straight. "Okay then, Sam. Okay. Truth of it is maybe it did mean something."

When she rolls into the room a second later, Claire is panting, her face shiny with perspiration. She has heard enough of the conversation to understand what has occurred.

Chick moves aside so she can bring her chair close to her father.

"You had a nightmare, didn't you?"

"No. It was more than that."

"Why don't you tell me about it."

Chick steps toward the doorway.

"Thank you, Chick," Claire says. She takes her father's hand in hers.

After he's composed himself, Sam tells his daughter about the dream. When he's finished, he says, "It was more than a dream, wasn't it?" He searches her eyes for an answer.

She squeezes his hand and whispers to him, the way she might whisper to a frightened child, the way he must have whispered to her when she was young and afraid after an upsetting dream. "It was just a dream," she says, and her eyes fill with tears. "It was just a bad dream." She remains by her father's side, his hand in hers, until she's certain he's fallen back to sleep, and then for a little while longer.

PART FOUR

CHAPTER 67

Sam

AFTER THAT FINAL UNSPEAKABLE nightmare, the visions gradually began to fade, and along with the visions, the sense of urgency that had been driving me since their inception. And my back too seems to improve just a little with each passing day. The belief that I could somehow rescue this stranger has passed as mysteriously as it came and the urgency and anxiety have been replaced by a sad, reluctant acceptance. My heart tells me that he will survive, and I hope I'm not mistaken, that I'm not just telling myself that to quash the guilt I might otherwise feel for abandoning him.

Since that horrific dream, my life has undergone numerous changes. I am living here, a permanent resident in the rural outskirts of Scranton now, with Claire. I wish I could explain it, how I came to be here, in this house, in this life that seems so far from what I once was, or thought I was, but is so near now to my heart. I believed I was coming to rescue someone, and instead I found a home. At times it seems I'm the one who's been rescued.

Perhaps Chick was the true wizard. How did he know what he seemed to know, how could he have understood what I still don't understand? Was I always the one in need of rescue? And as long as I am entertaining unanswerable questions, is this woman in this house the girl of whom I dreamed? If she's not, why would she take me in and treat me like a member of her family? Why does she seem to care so very deeply about an odd old man? Man or god or wizard or lunatic, I have little to offer. And yet I feel welcome here, more welcome even than I did with Chick, whom I came to love like a brother, more welcome than I have ever felt in any life I dare allow myself to recall. Perhaps this is the dream. Or perhaps we are all a part of one another, bound by our flaws as well as our humanity.

What I did, what I was, and what I felt before all of this is only an evanescent mist now, a wispy memory lacking substance or weight, a diaphanous feather drifting slowly away on some temperamental breeze. That is my choice.

CHAPTER 68

Chick

WELL I'LL BE DAMNED IF Sam didn't someway up and slip that shiny old chrome Zippo right into my pocket when he give me that long goodbye hug. She didn't care none for smoking, so I don't figure he'd have much usage for it anyways. Still in all, he must of somehow remembered I was interested. It was just like the one I had when I was a kid.

Fact of it is, I got a pretty fair idea she come to trust me too in the end there. Claire, I mean. I stayed on with the two of them for a couple weeks more, but it didn't take all that long to realize it when I wasn't much needed no more, and it was something of a relief. Funny thing is, when I told her I was heading on out, she give me quite a surprise. Why, she up and asked me if I'd care to stay on there with the two of them in definite. Said she'd just as soon have me around the house to entertain her father while she's off at work as out on the street somewheres eating stale leftovers and terrorizing the law-abiding citizens and the like. Course I knew she was just trying to be nice. She even offered to help me get fixed up with a job at that school of hers if I so desired it. Me, in a school. I guess I was tempted for about a minute or two, but the truth is I got no business taking nothing else from her. I sure as shit don't need no more reason than I already got to feel guilty.

203

That's a whole lot of weight to carry around and I'm getting older and kind of tired, truth is. And anyways, it didn't seem like there was nothing left for me to do around there.

She *did* say I was welcome back any time I got it in my head, but I can't see where that'd make any kind of sense neither. I don't figure none of us needs a daily reminder of how we all got to be what we are. Leastwise I know *I* don't. And no matter how much it might of changed, that house still had too many ugly memories for my purposes.

Sure, I suppose maybe I did do some kind of good, in a little way. Fact of it is I did try and help old Sam, and her too, for that matter. But like I always tend to say, that don't much change what I am nor what I done. Now I ain't going to say I don't feel glad about taking him back home to his daughter, but the way I got it figured, the worst of the damage I done can't be undid by good intents nor good deeds neither. True fact of it is she's still in a wheelchair, Sam's still loony as a jaybird, and the rest of that poor family is still dead and buried. Ain't none of that never going to change and I ain't about to start lying to myself about it now. I'm too old and tired for that kind of horseshit.

Anyways, I'm thinking on trying to get me some kind of work, at least for temporary. Course then I'd maybe want to head further south first and find me some warmer climes, so to say. These old bones has got brittle, and I don't care if I don't never see another goddamn flake of snow. Maybe it's true what they say about all them snowflakes being different, one from the other, but you can't prove it by me. Truth is I don't see how that makes a damn bit of difference if you ain't got a good unventilated pair of shoes to keep your feet warm and dry while you're out there running your comparisons. Who the hell's got that kind of time?

CHAPTER 69

Claire

AFTER ALL IS SAID AND DONE, I suppose we learn to live with what little we can squeeze out of life. I believe that's what they mean by acceptance. Of course, if you're happy, healthy, and secure, what you feel you can't live without is worlds different from what you think you need if you're lying in a gutter, crippled, starving, and cold. My goodness, I think Chick said something like that once.

As much as I wanted it, and I wanted it so very, very much, I don't believe I ever expected to see my father again, though I would have given anything I had just to know he was alive. But when I finally saw him standing on my doorstep, everything changed. Knowing he was alive was wonderful, but when I realized what came along with it I found that it was no longer enough. I couldn't imagine not having all of him, his heart, his mind, that familial bond. The idea of having him next to me, in my home, but being unable to tell him how much I'd missed him, how very much I loved him . . . how much I *love* him, was not one I was equipped to accept. The thought of having him here, but never being able to hear him say "I love you" was as painful then as all of the uncertainty had been only minutes before.

But life isn't here to satisfy our needs. I've had no choice but to accept what he is, with all the limitations. And though it isn't always easy, I have come to realize that this, what I have now, is really so much better, worlds better than wondering if he was dead or alive, if he was suffering or living a happy life with some new family.

As odd as it may sound, we continue to get a little closer every day, and even with all of his illusions, and with his peculiar manner, which has gradually mellowed, I love my father as much as I ever did. Perhaps more. And I am convinced that he has come to love me in his way, though he is too shy, too unsure of himself, I think, to ever put it into words. When we are together, we talk about life, about the stars and planets, and about the books we read. We do sweet little things for each other and sometimes we just spend our time together sitting in the living room, sharing a silent affection, an unspoken bond. At least that's how it feels to me, and I choose to believe that's what it is. If I am wrong, I don't care to know it.

The two of us are like a pair of timid dancers, caught up in an endless dance, never quite touching, each responsive to the other's moves, careful to leave enough space so that the other can travel freely about a stage made up of the fragile intersection of our souls without the awkwardness and discomfort, the hesitations, the missteps actual contact might engender.

CHAPTER 70

Sam

I TRY TO DO MY PART IN this relationship we've forged. I do whatever I can to help her keep the house in order, and I do my best to be a comfort to her, and to show her that I care for her. And it's never a chore. The truth is that there is great love between us, not the romantic love of a man and a woman, of course, but the love that two people with a special bond sometimes share, the love of family. And in some unexpected way, through paths neither of us would have chosen, that is what we have become. My life is far better, far fuller for her presence in it, and I am eternally grateful. There is my eternity.

CHAPTER 71

Claire

SOMETIMES LATE AT NIGHT, when he's sleeping and I'm still rattling around up here in my room, my mind abuzz with all that we've been through, I slip quietly into his room and sit close to him, watching his weather-beaten face. And sometimes, when he's been still for a time and I'm certain he's asleep, I whisper to him, "I love you. I love you, Daddy. Welcome home." And every now and then, as I turn to leave the room, I can almost convince myself that I see a hint of a smile wash softly over his ashen features, like a gentle spring rain washing over the distant Pennsylvania hills.

CHAPTER 72

Chick

CRAZY AS IT MAYBE SOUNDS, I got me a actual job in a little old general store in a sleepy country town down here in Southern Maryland. I guess I been here for coming on two years now, and truth is, I like it pretty good. Mary . . . I mean to say Mrs. Kresge, she pays me off the books, cause I ain't got no legal papers or such as that. Her husband up and died a couple five or six years ago, and she says she was kind of in over her head, what with running the business and ordering stuff and keeping the books and helping the customers and such as that. Maybe with that wild eye and all you might not think she's all that much to look at, and she's a couple few years older than me, but I figure I could do worse for a card-playing companion. She got her own peculiar ways, and she don't let me get away with no drinking whatsoever, but I got the run of the place, and plus which she's a pretty good listener and a damn good cook too. Maybe I'll stick around this time. Sure as hell ain't nowhere else I got to be anytime soon. Truth of it is I ain't all that sure I'd go if there was. Almost feels like home, I guess you could say. Who would of figured it? It's more than I deserve.

CHAPTER 73

Sam

HOW LONG HAS IT BEEN NOW? Two years? Three? Longer still? It's been long enough for me to know that I belong here. Long enough for me to understand that I am finally home.

Oh yes, I hear what she whispers to me late at night when she thinks I'm asleep. I hear her, and I know. Still, I guess there are some things you're better off never speaking about, never confronting face-to-face. The silence seems to somehow keep us safe from things that are still just too awful to say, that most likely will always be. Certainly I've gained something precious in learning how much I lost. And yet this life we've forged from the remnants of what might have been is so terribly precarious, fragile as a fallen leaf, brown and brittle with decay. I know I can never visit the graves, and I fear the words, were I brave enough or fool enough to utter them, might destroy us both, rending the blade from the veins, and crushing the remains until there's nothing left but formless flakes and dust, subject to the slightest breeze. But how could I not know? After all, she is my daughter. She is my dear, beloved child.

PART FIVE

Mary—About Four Years Later

SOMETIMES MAYBE YOU don't know it, but you already have everything you need. At least that's what it seems like to me now.

I stood some distance away at first, just watching them for a while, trying to get some kind of feeling about them, I guess. Course I knew it was them, what with her in that wheelchair and him looking old and more than a little worn out. Anyways, I couldn't think of anybody else would be paying their respects to him. Once we got to talking, they seemed like nice enough folks, which was really no surprise after I knew how Barry felt about them. He would of done anything for them, either one. The old guy was awful quiet and maybe just a bit on the peculiar side, but then I imagine you could call me peculiar too. I don't doubt some folks do. His daughter seemed more normal, but maybe kind of sad and a little shy underneath.

I was disappointed at first, I mean when I realized they weren't going to tell me anything I didn't already know. But now that they're gone back home and I've had some time to think on it, I'm glad. They were trying to do me a favor and I got a feeling they did exactly right. See, what I've come to understand is it doesn't much matter. There was something gnawing at him and that's for sure, but I can't think of a thing in the world that would alter my opinion of him anyway, and if there *is* something, I can't see now what good it would do me or anyone else to know what that thing is.

Here's what I do know. I know the man never stole a penny from me from the first day I let him run the register until the day he died. I know he . . . he loved me. I could see it in his face, hear it in his voice when he told me again how he didn't deserve me. I know he made me feel cared for, appreciated, even cherished, things a woman needs. I know he cried for a day and a night when my old dog Jim died and that he went out early next morning and got me a new dog and that although he knew a new dog wouldn't ease the pain he also knew it was the only thing he could do and that doing nothing wasn't an option. The man I married was rough around the edges, sure, but he was gentle and kind like no other man I've known, and I guess I've known a few.

I suppose I'll be content to hang on to the man I'm familiar with, the one I can recognize, the one makes me feel real damn lucky for having known him, the one makes me feel honored that, by God, he loved me. Me! Like I said, sometimes maybe you don't know it, but you already have everything you need. It's true, it makes me feel good to think about that quirky outcast I married so late in life, and if that's a sin, well then I suppose I'm just an old sinner. There are most likely worse things than hell. And he was pretty sure he'd find his way there anyway. Long as we end up together, I imagine we'll find some way to deal with the heat.

Acknowledgements

I WANT TO EXPRESS MY APPRECIATION for those extraordinary readers who possess the imagination to immerse themselves in literature— rather than merely consume it—and the curiosity to explore its penetralia.

Without these people there would be little reason to write.

I'd also like to thank Crystal, Lauren, Brooke, and the entire SparkPress team for their patience and support, and the multitalented Julie Metz for yet another outstanding cover.

About The Author

Originally from northeastern Pennsylvania, GRANT JARRETT lived in Manhattan for twenty years before moving to Marin County, CA, where he now works as a writer, ghostwriter, editor, musician, and occasional songwriter. His publishing credits include numerous magazine articles, essays, short stories, and *More Towels*, his coming-of-age memoir about life on the road. His debut novel, *Ways of Leaving*, won the Best New Fiction category in the 2014 International Book Awards. *The House That Made Me*, his 2016 anthology about the meaning of home, was chosen as an *Elle* "Trust Us" book. Jarrett is an avid cyclist, skier, and surf skier.

Selected Titles from SparkPress

SparkPress is an independent boutique publisher delivering high-quality, entertaining, and engaging content that enhances readers' lives, with a special focus on female-driven work. Visit us at www.gosparkpress.com

The House That Made Me, by Grant Jarrett. $17, 978-1-94071-631-2. In this candid, evocative collection of essays, a diverse group of acclaimed authors reflects on the diverse homes, neighborhoods, and experiences that helped shape them—using Google Earth software to revisit the location in the process. Moving and life-affirming, this poignant anthology gives fresh insight into the concept of Home.

The Year of Necessary Lies, by Kris Radish. $17, 978-1-94071-651-0. A great-granddaughter discovers her ancestor's secrets—inspirational forays into forbidden love and the Florida Everglades at the turn of the last century.

Hindsight, by Mindy Tarquini, $16.95, 978-1943006014. Eugenia Panisporchi, a thirty-three-year-old Chaucer professor who remembers all her past lives, is desperate to change her future. Her hope is that the Blessed Virgin Mary (who oversees her soul's progress) will grant her heart's desire, the option to choose the circumstances of her next life. But when a student reveals he shares her ability, Eugenia suddenly finds herself setting up a Facebook page and sponsoring a support group for others like her, and she discovers she must confront her current shortcomings before she can break the cycle and finally live the life of her dreams.

Ways of Leaving, by Grant Jarrett. $15, 978-1-94071-641-1. Following the death of his father, the loss of his job, and the failure of his marriage, Chase Stoller returns home to try to reconstruct his life. But bad habits, like alcoholism, sex addiction, and poor impulse control, make his homecoming as problematic as his screwed-up life.

The Absence of Evelyn, Jackie Townsend. $16.95, 978-1-94300-621-2. Nineteen-year-old Olivia's life takes a turn when she receives an overseas call from a man she doesn't know is her father; her mother Rhonda, meanwhile, haunted by her sister's ghost, must face long-buried truths.

About SparkPress

SPARKPRESS IS AN INDEPENDENT, hybrid imprint focused on merging the best of the traditional publishing model with new and innovative strategies. We deliver high-quality, entertaining, and engaging content that enhances readers' lives. We are proud to bring to market a list of *New York Times* best-selling, award-winning, and debut authors who represent a wide array of genres, as well as our established, industry-wide reputation for creative, results-driven success in working with authors. SparkPress, a BookSparks imprint, is a division of SparkPoint Studio LLC.

Learn more at GoSparkPress.com